SOMEHOW
TENDERNESS
SURVIVES

Litterary Terms

<u>Forshadowing</u> - provides hints of what's to come

<u>Personification</u> - assign human charactaristi to an inanimate object

<u>Pathetic Fallacy</u> - a greater form of personification

pathetic comes from the word "pathos"

SOMEHOW TENDERNESS SURVIVES

Stories of Southern Africa

SELECTED BY

HAZEL ROCHMAN

A Charlotte Zolotow Book

HarperKeypoint
An Imprint of HarperCollins*Publishers*

Somehow Tenderness Survives: Stories of Southern Africa
Copyright © 1988 by Hazel Rochman

Library of Congress Cataloging-in-Publication Data

Somehow tenderness survives : stories of southern Africa / selected by
Hazel Rochman.—1st ed.
    p.   cm.
"A Charlotte Zolotow book."
Summary: A collection of ten short stories about southern Africa—
five by black southern Africans and five by white southern Africans.
    ISBN 0-06-025022-4
    ISBN 0-06-025023-2 (lib. bdg.)
    1. South Africa—Juvenile fiction.   2. Short stories, South
African (English)
    [1. South Africa—Fiction.   2. Short stories.]   I. Rochman, Hazel.
PZ5.S695   1988   88–916
[Fic]—dc19   CIP
                                                                                      AC

    ISBN 0-06-447063-6 (pbk.)

Hazel Rochman's royalties for this book are being donated to an anti-
apartheid organization.

I am grateful to my friend and colleague Rita Headrick, 1942–88, African scholar and Social Studies teacher at the University of Chicago Laboratory Schools, who always used great stories to humanize history and politics. It was her request for "a story to show students what it's like to grow up under apartheid" that led to this anthology.

I have cherished the ideal of a democratic and free society in which all persons live together in harmony and with equal opportunities. It is an ideal which I hope to live for and to achieve. But if needs be, it is an ideal for which I am prepared to die.

—Nelson Mandela, leader of the African National Congress.

[1964, Rivonia trial, before being sentenced to life in prison.]

[And again in 1990, Cape Town, upon his release after twenty-seven years.]

SOMEHOW WE SURVIVE

Dennis Brutus

Somehow we survive
and tenderness, frustrated, does not wither.

Investigating searchlights rake
our naked unprotected contours;

over our heads the monolithic decalogue
of fascist prohibition glowers
and teeters for a catastrophic fall;

boots club the peeling door.

But somehow we survive
severance, deprivation, loss.

Patrols uncoil along the asphalt dark
hissing their menace to our lives,

most cruel, all our land is scarred with terror,
rendered unlovely and unlovable;
sundered are we and all our passionate
    surrender

but somehow tenderness survives.

Contents

Introduction   3

Crackling Day   7
  Peter Abrahams

The Old Chief Mshlanga   23
  Doris Lessing

A Day in the Country   46
  Dan Jacobson

Country Lovers   61
  Nadine Gordimer

When the Train Comes   76
  Zoë Wicomb

The Toilet   98
  Gcina Mhlope

The Road to Alexandra   111
  Mark Mathabane

A Chip of Glass Ruby   135
   Nadine Gordimer

A Farm at Raraba   153
   Ernst Havemann

It's Quiet Now   175
   Gcina Mhlope

Glossary   179

Notes on Contributors   183

Acknowledgments   187

SOMEHOW
TENDERNESS
SURVIVES

Sources for Facts and Statistics:

"Apartheid's violence against children." Working paper for International Conference on Children, Repression and the Law in Apartheid South Africa. Harare, Zimbabwe, September 1987. (Prepared with the assistance of the International Defence & Aid Fund for Southern Africa.)

Butts, Cassandra. "South Africa: Children under Attack." *TransAfrica News*, Volume 6, Number 3; Summer 1987.

"Children in Detention in South Africa: Fact Sheet." Southern Africa Project of the Lawyers' Committee for Civil Rights under Law. Washington, 1987.

Coleman, Audrey. "Children in Detention in South Africa." United Nations Centre against Apartheid. July 1987. (Ms. Coleman is a founding member of the Johannesburg-based Detainees' Parents Support Committee. The government banned The Committee in 1988.)

"South Africa Fact Sheet." December 1986. The Africa Fund (associated with the American Committee on Africa).

Survey of Race Relations in South Africa. Annual. South African Institute of Race Relations, Johannesburg.

The Weekly Mail. WM Publications, Johannesburg.

Forshadowing
Personification } litterary terms
Pathetic Fallacy

Introduction

Coming of age under apartheid involves violence and suffering. Blacks know hunger, prison, family separation, and exile as common experience.

Black children are fourteen to fifteen times more likely to die before the age of five than white children. Approximately 3 million black children suffer from malnutrition— in one of the richest countries in the world.

Where racism is the law:

• Blacks may not vote, and they may not live or work where they choose.

• The migrant labor system forces fathers to leave their families.

• Black education is separate and inferior to white.

• The police and army can hold anyone—in-cluding children—indefinitely and secretly without trial and without charge. No one may campaign for the release of detainees. They do not have the right of access to family, lawyers, or their own doctors.

• Only restricted media coverage of unrest is allowed.

The official use of language is reminiscent of Orwell's Newspeak, where jargon hides the truth. Most grotesque is "homelands," the name for the barren and alien rural areas where millions of blacks have been forcibly resettled with no work and little food, shelter, and medical care.

Apartheid's meaning cannot be disguised, though. The Afrikaans word means "separateness." It's pronounced "apart-hate."

These stories and autobiographical accounts, written by southern African writers of various races over the last 35 years, humanize the statistics and expose the Newspeak. They reveal, as powerful literature can, the complex individual experience beneath the banal cliché. Their passion is tightly controlled, often understated. Shack, kitchen, slum, suburb, farm, and open veld are the settings for intense moments when characters move beyond stereotype to surprise you.

The politics of racism deeply affect personal identity. These stories show how it feels when you are black and the police break down the door of your home in a midnight raid and drag your father to prison because his papers aren't in order. Or when they punish you for defying a white bully; or for loving someone of another color.

A mixed-race teenager takes the rare chance of a superior education in a white school, and finds loneliness and self-hatred.

A black girl living illegally with her maidservant sister in a white area can find privacy only in a public toilet.

A township resident recognizes seething rebellion and police violence as a part of daily life.

After she's fed her family, a traditional Indian woman prints illegal political pamphlets on her duplicating machine to support the African workers' strike.

An Afrikaans soldier and a black guerrilla on the border talk through the night and then return to war and torture.

For one white boy, growing up can mean violating the best in himself so that he can fit in with white supremacy. For another, guilt corrupts relationships with family and neighbors. For a few whites, coming of age may be the opposite of acceptance: It may be the sudden realization that a black is a *person* or the slow dawning of the terrible knowledge that the moral universe you have always taken for granted is evil.

The stories are grim; but they speak of courage and tenderness in daily life, even where home has become a public toilet or a prison cell.

Hazel Rochman
1988

"It's about suffering.
How to end suffering.
And it ends in suffering. Yes, it's strange to live in a country where there are still heroes."
(from *Burger's Daughter* by Nadine Gordimer)

Crackling Day

Peter Abrahams

[handwritten: Hunger]

[handwritten: abase—to humble or degrade]
[handwritten: abase→baseus→low]
[handwritten: abasing beginning; no "I" until third sentence]

Wednesday was crackling day. On that day the children of the location made the long trek to Elsburg siding for the square of pig's rind that passed for our daily meat. We collected a double lot of cow dung the day before; a double lot of mocroga.

[handwritten: Forshadowing]

I finished my breakfast and washed up. Aunt Liza was at her washtub in the yard. A misty, sickly sun was just showing. And on the open veld the frost lay thick and white on the grass.

"Ready?" Aunt Liza called.

I went out to her. She shook the soapsuds off her swollen hands and wiped them on her apron. She lifted the apron and put her hand through the slits of the many thin cotton dresses she wore. The dress nearest the skin was the one with the pocket. From this she pulled a sixpenny piece.

7

She tied it in a knot on the corner of a bit of coloured cloth and handed it to me.

"Take care of that. . . . Take the smaller piece of bread in the bin, but don't eat it till you start back. You can have a small piece of crackling with it. Only a small piece, understand?"

"Yes, Aunt Liza."

"All right."

I got the bread and tucked it into the little canvas bag in which I would carry the crackling.

"'Bye, Aunt Liza." I trotted off, one hand in my pocket, feeling the cloth where the money was. I paused at Andries's home.

"Andries!" I danced up and down while I waited. The cold was not so terrible on bare feet if one did not keep still.

Andries came trotting out of his yard. His mother's voice followed, desperate and plaintive:

"I'll skin you if you lose the money!"

"Women!" Andries said bitterly.

I glimpsed the dark, skinny woman at her wash-tub as we trotted across the veld. Behind and in front of us, other children trotted in twos and threes.

There was a sharp bite to the morning air I sucked in; it stung my nose so that tears came to my eyes; it went down my throat like an icy draught; my nose ran. I tried breathing through my mouth, but this was worse. The cold went through my shirt and shorts; my skin went pimply and chilled; my fingers went numb and began to ache; my feet felt like frozen lumps that did not belong to me, yet jarred and hurt each time I put them down. I began to feel sick and desperate.

"Jesus God in heaven!" Andries cried suddenly.

I looked at him. His eyes were rimmed in red. Tears ran down his cheeks. His face was drawn and purple, a sick look on it.

"Faster," I said.

"Think it'll help?"

I nodded. We went faster. We passed two children, sobbing and moaning as they ran. We were all in the same desperate situation. We were creatures haunted and hounded by the cold. It was a cruel enemy who gave no quarter. And our means of fighting it were pitifully inadequate. In all the mornings and evenings of the winter months, young and old, big and small, were helpless victims of the bitter cold. Only toward noon and in the early afternoon, when the sun sat high in the sky, was there a brief respite. For us, the children, the cold, especially the morning cold, assumed an awful and malevolent personality. We talked of "it." "It" was a half-human monster with evil thoughts, evil intentions, bent on destroying us. "It" was happiest when we were most miserable. Andries had told me how "it" had, last winter, caught and killed a boy.

Hunger was an enemy too, but one with whom we could come to terms, who had many virtues and values. Hunger gave our pap, *moeroga*, and crackling a feastlike quality. When it was not with us, we could think and talk kindly about it. Its memory could even give moments of laughter. But the cold of winter was with us all the time. "It" never really eased up. There were only more bearable degrees of "it" at high noon and on mild days. "It" was the real enemy. And on this Wednesday morning, as we ran across the veld, winter was more bitterly, bitingly, freezingly real than ever.

The sun climbed. The frozen earth thawed, leaving the short grass looking wet and weary. Painfully our feet and legs came alive. The aching numbness slowly left our fingers. We ran more slowly in the more bearable cold.

In climbing, the sun lost some of its damp look and seemed a real, if cold, sun. When it was right overhead, we struck the sandy road, which meant we were nearing the siding. None of the others were in sight. Andries and I were alone on the sandy road on the open veld. We slowed down to a brisk walk. We were sufficiently thawed to want to talk.

"How far?" I said.

"A few minutes," he said.

"I've got a piece of bread," I said.

"Me too," he said. "Let's eat it now."

"On the way back," I said. "With a bit of crackling."

"Good idea. . . . Race to the fork."

"All right."

"Go!" he said.

We shot off together, legs working like pistons. He soon pulled away from me. He reached the fork in the road some fifty yards ahead.

"I win!" he shouted gleefully, though his teeth still chattered.

We pitched stones down the road, each trying to pitch farther than the other. I won and wanted to go on doing it. But Andries soon grew weary with pitching. We raced again. Again he won. He wanted another race, but I refused. I wanted pitching, but he refused. So, sulking with each other, we reached the pig farm.

We followed a fenced-off pathway round sprawling white buildings. Everywhere about us was the grunt of pigs. As we passed an open doorway, a huge dog came bounding out, snarling and barking at us. In our terror we forgot it was fenced in, and we streaked away. Surprised, I found myself a good distance ahead of Andries. We looked back and saw a young white woman call the dog to heel.

"Damn Boer dog," Andries said.

"Matter with it?" I asked.

"They teach them to go for us. Never get caught by one. My old man's got a hole in his bottom where a Boer dog got him."

I remembered I had outstripped him.

"I won!" I said.

"Only because you were frightened," he said.

"I still won."

"Scare arse," he jeered.

"Scare arse, yourself!"

"I'll knock you!"

"I'll knock you back!"

A couple of white men came down the path and ended our possible fight. We hurried past them to the distant shed where a line had already formed. There were grown-ups and children. All the grown-ups and some of the children were from places other than our location.

The line moved slowly. The young white man who served us did it in leisurely fashion, with long pauses for a smoke. Occasionally he turned his back.

At last, after what seemed hours, my turn came. Andries was behind me. I took the sixpenny piece from the square of cloth and offered it to the man.

"Well?" he said.

"Sixpence crackling, please."

Andries nudged me in the back. The man's stare suddenly became cold and hard. Andries whispered into my ear.

"Well?" the man repeated coldly.

"Please, *baas*," I said.

"What d'you want?"

"Sixpence crackling, please."

"What?"

Andries dug me in the ribs.

"Sixpence crackling, please."

"What?"

"Sixpence crackling, please, *baas*."

"You new here?"

"Yes, *baas*." I looked at his feet while he stared at me.

At last he took the sixpenny piece from me. I held my bag open while he filled it with crackling from a huge pile on a large canvas sheet on the ground. Turning away, I stole a fleeting glance at his face. His eyes met mine, and there was amused, challenging mockery in them. I waited for Andries at the back of the line, out of the reach of the white man's mocking eyes.

The cold day was at its mildest as we walked home along the sandy road. I took out my piece of bread and, with a small piece of greasy crackling, still warm, on it, I munched as we went along. We had not yet made our peace, so Andries munched his bread and crackling on the other side of the road.

"Dumb fool!" he mocked at me for <u>not knowing how to address</u> the white man.

"Scare arse!" I shouted back.

Thus, hurling curses at each other, we reached the fork. Andries saw them first and moved over to my side of the road.

"White boys," he said.

There were three of them, two of about our own size and one slightly bigger. They had school bags and were coming toward us up the road from the siding.

"Better run for it," Andries said.

"Why?"

"No, that'll draw them. Let's just walk along, but quickly."

"Why?" I repeated.

"Shut up," he said.

Some of his anxiety touched me. Our own scrap was forgotten. We marched side by side as fast as we could. The white boys saw us and hurried up the road. We passed the fork. Perhaps they would take the turning away from us. We dared not look back.

"Hear them?" Andries asked.

"No." I looked over my shoulder. "They're coming," I said.

"Walk faster," Andries said. "If they come closer, run."

"Hey, *klipkop!*"

"Don't look back," Andries said.

"Hottentot!"

We walked as fast as we could.

"Bloody kaffir!"

Ahead was a bend in the road. Behind the bend were bushes. Once there, we could run without them knowing it till it was too late.

"Faster," Andries said.

They began pelting us with stones.

"Run when we get to the bushes," Andries said.

The bend and the bushes were near. We would soon be there.

A clear young voice carried to us: "Your fathers are dirty black bastards of baboons!"

"Run!" Andries called.

A violent, unreasoning anger suddenly possessed me. I stopped and turned.

"You're a liar!" I screamed it.

The foremost boy pointed at me. "An ugly black baboon!"

In a fog of rage I went toward him.

"Liar!" I shouted. "My father was better than your father!"

I neared them. The bigger boy stepped between me and the one I was after.

"My father was better than your father! Liar!"

The big boy struck me a mighty clout on the side of the face. I staggered, righted myself, and leaped at the boy who had insulted my father. I struck him on the face, hard. A heavy blow on the back of my head nearly stunned me. I grabbed at the boy in front of me. We went down together.

"Liar!" I said through clenched teeth, hitting him with all my might.

Blows rained on me—on my head, my neck, the side of my face, my mouth—but my enemy was under me and I pounded him fiercely, all the time repeating:

"Liar! Liar! Liar!"

Suddenly stars exploded in my head. Then there was darkness.

I emerged from the darkness to find Andries kneeling beside me.

"God, man! I thought they'd killed you."

I sat up. The white boys were nowhere to be seen. Like Andries, they'd probably thought me dead and run off in panic. The inside of my mouth felt sore and swollen. My nose was tender to the touch. The back of my head ached. A trickle of blood dripped from my nose. I stemmed it with the square of coloured cloth. The greatest damage was to my shirt. It was ripped in many places. I remembered the crackling. I looked anxiously about. It was safe, a little off the road on the grass. I relaxed. I got up and brushed my clothes. I picked up the crackling.

"God, you're dumb!" Andries said. "You're going to get it! Dumb arse!"

I was too depressed to retort. Besides, I knew he was right. I was dumb. I should have run when he told me to.

"Come on," I said.

One of many small groups of children, each child carrying his little bag of crackling, we trod the long road home in the cold winter afternoon.

There was tension in the house that night. When I got back, Aunt Liza had listened to the story in silence. The beating or scolding I expected did not come. But Aunt Liza changed while she listened, became remote and withdrawn. When Uncle Sam came home she told him what had happened. He, too, just looked at me and became more remote and withdrawn than usual. They were waiting for something; their tension reached out to me, and I waited with them, anxious, apprehensive.

The thing we waited for came while we were having our supper. We heard a trap pull up outside.

"Here it is," Uncle Sam said, and got up.

Aunt Liza leaned back from the table and put her hands in her lap, fingers intertwined, a cold, unseeing look in her eyes.

Before Uncle Sam reached the door, it burst open. A tall, broad, white man strode in. Behind him came the three boys. The one I had attacked had swollen lips and a puffy left eye.

"Evening, *baas*," Uncle Sam murmured.

"That's him," the bigger boy said, pointing at me.

The white man stared till I lowered my eyes.

"Well?" he said.

"He's sorry, *baas*," Uncle Sam said quickly. "I've given him a hiding he won't forget soon.

You know how it is, *baas*. He's new here, the child of a relative in Johannesburg, and they don't all know how to behave there. You know how it is in the big towns, *baas*." The plea in Uncle Sam's voice had grown more pronounced as he went on. He turned to me. "Tell the *baas* and young *basies* how sorry you are, Lee."

I looked at Aunt Liza and something in her lifelessness made me stubborn in spite of my fear.

"He insulted my father," I said.

The white man smiled.

"See, Sam, your hiding couldn't have been good."

There was a flicker of life in Aunt Liza's eyes. For a brief moment she saw me, looked at me, warmly, lovingly; then her eyes went dead again.

"He's only a child, *baas*," Uncle Sam murmured.

"You stubborn too, Sam?"

"No, *baas*."

"Good. Then teach him, Sam. If you and he are to live here, you must teach him. Well—?"

"Yes, *baas*."

Uncle Sam went into the other room and returned with a thick leather thong. He wound it once round his hand and advanced on me. The man and the boys leaned against the door, watching. I looked at Aunt Liza's face. Though there was no sign of life or feeling on it, I knew, suddenly, instinctively, that she wanted me not to cry.

Bitterly, Uncle Sam said: "You must never lift your hand to a white person. No matter what happens, you must never lift your hand to a white person. . . ."

He lifted the strap and brought it down on my back. I clenched my teeth and stared at Aunt Liza. I did not cry with the first three strokes. Then, suddenly, Aunt Liza went limp. Tears showed in her eyes. The thong came down on my back again and again. I screamed and begged for mercy. I groveled at Uncle Sam's feet, begging him to stop, promising never to lift my hand to any white person. . . .

At last the white man's voice said: "All right, Sam."

Uncle Sam stopped. I lay whimpering on the floor. Aunt Liza sat like one in a trance.

"Is he still stubborn, Sam?"

"Tell the *baas* and *basies* you are sorry."

"I'm sorry," I said.

"Bet his father is one of those who believe in equality."

"His father is dead," Aunt Liza said.

"Good night, Sam."

"Good night, *baas*. Sorry about this."

"All right, Sam." He opened the door. The boys went out first, then he followed. "Good night, Liza."

Aunt Liza did not answer. The door shut behind the white folk, and soon we heard their trap moving away. Uncle Sam flung the thong viciously against the door, slumped down on the bench, folded his arms on the table, and buried his head on his arms. Aunt Liza moved away from him, sat down on the floor beside me, and lifted me into her large lap. She sat rocking my body. Uncle Sam began to sob softly. After some time he raised his head and looked at us.

"Explain to the child, Liza," he said.

"You explain," Aunt Liza said bitterly. "You are the man. You did the beating. You are the head of the family. This is a man's world. You do the explaining."

"Please, Liza."

"You should be happy. The whites are satisfied. We can go on now."

With me in her arms, Aunt Liza got up. She carried me into the other room. The food on the table remained half eaten. She laid me on the bed on my stomach, smeared fat on my back, then covered me with the blankets. She undressed and got into bed beside me. She cuddled me close, warmed me with her own body. With her big hand on my cheek, she rocked me, first to silence, then to sleep.

For the only time during my stay there, I slept on a bed in Elsburg.

When I woke next morning, Uncle Sam had gone. Aunt Liza only once referred to the beating he had given me. It was in the late afternoon, when I returned with the day's cow dung.

"It hurt him," she said. "You'll understand one day."

That night Uncle Sam brought me an orange, a bag of boiled sweets, and a dirty old picture book. He smiled as he gave them to me, rather anxiously. When I smiled back at him, he seemed to relax. He put his hand on my head, started to say something, then changed his mind and took his seat by the fire.

Aunt Liza looked up from the floor, when she dished out the food.

"It's all right, old man," she murmured.

"One day . . ." Uncle Sam said.

"It's all right," Aunt Liza repeated insistently.

The Old Chief Mshlanga

Doris Lessing

They were good, the years of ranging the bush over her father's farm, which, like every white farm, was largely unused, broken only occasionally by small patches of cultivation. In between, nothing but trees, the long sparse grass, thorn and cactus and gully, grass and outcrop and thorn. And a jutting piece of rock which had been thrust up from the warm soil of Africa unimaginable eras of time ago, washed into hollows and whorls by sun and wind that had travelled so many thousands of miles of space and bush, would hold the weight of a small girl whose eyes were sightless for anything but a pale willowed river, a pale gleaming castle—a small girl singing: "Out flew the web and floated wide, the mirror cracked from side to side. . . ."

Pushing her way through the green aisles of the

Is she imagining?

23

mealie stalks, the leaves arching like cathedrals veined with sunlight far overhead, with the packed red earth underfoot, a fine lace of red starred witchweed would summon up a black bent figure croaking premonitions: the Northern witch, bred of cold Northern forests, would stand before her among the mealie fields, and it was the mealie fields that faded and fled, leaving her among the gnarled roots of an oak, snow falling thick and soft and white, the woodcutter's fire glowing red welcome through crowding tree trunks.

A white child, opening its eyes curiously on a sun-suffused landscape, a gaunt and violent landscape, might be supposed to accept it as her own, to take the msasa trees and the thorn trees as familiars, to feel her blood running free and responsive to the swing of the seasons.

This child could not see a msasa tree, or the thorn, for what they were. Her books held tales of alien fairies, her rivers ran slow and peaceful, and she knew the shape of the leaves of an ash or an oak, the names of the little creatures that lived in English streams, when the words "the veld" meant strangeness, though she could remember nothing else.

Because of this, for many years, it was the veld

that seemed unreal; the sun was a foreign sun, and the wind spoke a strange language.

The black people on the farm were as remote as the trees and the rocks. They were an amorphous black mass, mingling and thinning and massing like tadpoles, faceless, who existed merely to serve, to say "Yes, Baas," take their money and go. They changed season by season, moving from one farm to the next, according to their outlandish needs, which one did not have to understand, coming from perhaps hundreds of miles north or east, passing on after a few months—where? Perhaps even as far away as the fabled gold mines of Johannesburg, where the pay was so much better than the few shillings a month and the double handful of mealie meal twice a day which they earned in that part of Africa.

The child was taught to take them for granted: the servants in the house would come running a hundred yards to pick up a book if she dropped it. She was called "Nkosikaas"—Chieftainess— even by the black children her own age.

Later, when the farm grew too small to hold her curiosity, she carried a gun in the crook of her arm and wandered miles a day, from vlei to vlei, from *kopje* to *kopje*, accompanied by two dogs:

the dogs and the gun were an armour against fear. Because of them she never felt fear.

If a native came into sight along the kaffir paths half a mile away, the dogs would flush him up a tree as if he were a bird. If he expostulated (in his uncouth language, which was by itself ridiculous) that was cheek. If one was in a good mood, it could be a matter for laughter. Otherwise one passed on, hardly glancing at the angry man in the tree.

On the rare occasions when white children met together they could amuse themselves by hailing a passing native in order to make a buffoon of him; they could set the dogs on him and watch him run; they could tease a small black child as if he were a puppy—save that they would not throw stones and sticks at a dog without a sense of guilt.

Later still, certain questions presented themselves in the child's mind; and because the answers were not easy to accept, they were silenced by an even greater arrogance of manner.

It was even impossible to think of the black people who worked about the house as friends, for if she talked to one of them, her mother would come running anxiously: "Come away; you mustn't talk to natives."

It was this instilled consciousness of danger, of something unpleasant, that made it easy to laugh out loud, crudely, if a servant made a mistake in his English or if he failed to understand an order— there is a certain kind of laughter that is fear, afraid of itself.

One evening, when I was about fourteen, I was walking down the side of a mealie field that had been newly ploughed, so that the great red clods showed fresh and tumbling to the vlei beyond, like a choppy red sea; it was that hushed and listening hour, when the birds send long sad calls from tree to tree, and all the colours of earth and sky and leaf are deep and golden. I had my rifle in the curve of my arm, and the dogs were at my heels.

In front of me, perhaps a couple of hundred yards away, a group of three Africans came into sight around the side of a big antheap. I whistled the dogs close in to my skirts and let the gun swing in my hand, and advanced, waiting for them to move aside, off the path, in respect for my passing. But they came on steadily, and the dogs looked up at me for the command to chase. I was angry. It was "cheek" for a native not to stand off a path, the moment he caught sight of you.

In front walked an old man, stooping his weight

onto a stick, his hair grizzled white, a dark red blanket slung over his shoulders like a cloak. Behind him came two young men, carrying bundles of pots, assegais, hatchets.

The group was not a usual one. They were not natives seeking work. These had an air of dignity, of quietly following their own purpose. It was the dignity that checked my tongue. I walked quietly on, talking softly to the growling dogs, till I was ten paces away. Then the old man stopped, drawing his blanket close.

"Morning, Nkosikaas," he said, using the customary greeting for any time of the day.

"Good morning," I said. "Where are you going?" My voice was a little truculent.

The old man spoke in his own language, then one of the young men stepped forward politely and said in careful English: "My Chief travels to see his brothers beyond the river."

A Chief! I thought, understanding the pride that made the old man stand before me like an equal—more than an equal, for he showed courtesy, and I showed none.

The old man spoke again, wearing dignity like an inherited garment, still standing ten paces off, flanked by his entourage, not looking at me (that would have been rude) but directing his eyes somewhere over my head at the trees.

"You are the little Nkosikaas from the farm of Baas Jordan?"

"That's right," I said.

"Perhaps your father does not remember," said the interpreter for the old man, "but there was an affair with some goats. I remember seeing you when you were . . ." The young man held his hand at knee level and smiled.

We all smiled.

"What is your name?" I asked.

"This is Chief Mshlanga," said the young man.

"I will tell my father that I met you," I said.

The old man said: "My greetings to your father, little Nkosikaas."

"Good morning," I said politely, finding the politeness difficult, from lack of use.

"Morning, little Nkosikaas," said the old man, and stood aside to let me pass.

I went by, my gun hanging awkwardly, the dogs sniffing and growling, cheated of their favourite game of chasing natives like animals.

Not long afterwards I read in an old explorer's book the phrase: "Chief Mshlanga's country." It went like this: "Our destination was Chief

Mshlanga's country, to the north of the river; and it was our desire to ask his permission to prospect for gold in his territory."

The phrase "ask his permission" was so extraordinary to a white child, brought up to consider all natives as things to use, that it revived those questions, which could not be suppressed: they fermented slowly in my mind.

On another occasion one of those old prospectors who still move over Africa looking for neglected reefs, with their hammers and tents, and pans for sifting gold from crushed rock, came to the farm and, in talking of the old days, used that phrase again: "This was the Old Chief's country," he said. "It stretched from those mountains over there way back to the river, hundreds of miles of country." That was his name for our district: "The Old Chief's Country"; he did not use our name for it—a new phrase which held no implication of usurped ownership.

As I read more books about the time when this part of Africa was opened up, not much more than fifty years before, I found Old Chief Mshlanga had been a famous man, known to all the explorers and prospectors. But then he had been young; or maybe it was his father or uncle they spoke of—I never found out.

During that year I met him several times in the part of the farm that was traversed by natives moving over the country. I learned that the path up the side of the big red field where the birds sang was the recognized highway for migrants. Perhaps I even haunted it in the hope of meeting him: being greeted by him, the exchange of courtesies, seemed to answer the questions that troubled me.

Soon I carried a gun in a different spirit; I used it for shooting food and not to give me confidence. And now the dogs learned better manners. When I saw a native approaching, we offered and took greetings; and slowly that other landscape in my mind faded, and my feet struck directly on the African soil, and I saw the shapes of tree and hill clearly, and the black people moved back, as it were, out of my life: it was as if I stood aside to watch a slow intimate dance of landscape and men, a very old dance, whose steps I could not learn.

But I thought: this is my heritage, too; I was bred here; it is my country as well as the black man's country; and there is plenty of room for all of us, without elbowing each other off the pavements and roads.

It seemed it was only necessary to let free that

respect I felt when I was talking with old Chief Mshlanga, to let both black and white people meet gently, with tolerance for each other's differences: it seemed quite easy.

Then, one day, something new happened. Working in our house as servants were always three natives: cook, houseboy, garden boy. They used to change as the farm natives changed: staying for a few months, then moving on to a new job, or back home to their kraals. They were thought of as "good" or "bad" natives; which meant: how did they behave as servants? Were they lazy, efficient, obedient, or disrespectful? If the family felt good-humoured, the phrase was: "What can you expect from raw black savages?" If we were angry, we said: "These damned niggers, we would be much better off without them."

One day, a white policeman was on his rounds of the district, and he said laughingly: "Did you know you have an important man in your kitchen?"

"What!" exclaimed my mother sharply. "What do you mean?"

"A Chief's son." The policeman seemed amused. "He'll boss the tribe when the old man dies."

"He'd better not put on a Chief's son act with me," said my mother.

When the policeman left, we looked with different eyes at our cook: he was a good worker, but he drank too much at weekends—that was how we knew him.

He was a tall youth, with very black skin, like black polished metal, his tightly growing black hair parted white man's fashion at one side, with a metal comb from the store stuck into it; very polite, very distant, very quick to obey an order. Now that it had been pointed out, we said: "Of course, you can see. Blood always tells."

My mother became strict with him now she knew about his birth and prospects. Sometimes, when she lost her temper, she would say: "You aren't the Chief yet, you know." And he would answer her very quietly, his eyes on the ground: "Yes, Nkosikaas."

One afternoon he asked for a whole day off, instead of the customary half day, to go home next Sunday.

"How can you go home in one day?"

"It will take me half an hour on my bicycle," he explained.

I watched the direction he took; and the next

day I went off to look for this kraal; I understood he must be Chief Mshlanga's successor: there was no other kraal near enough our farm.

Beyond our boundaries on that side the country was new to me. I followed unfamiliar paths past *kopjes* that till now had been part of the jagged horizon, hazed with distance. This was Government land, which had never been cultivated by white men; at first I could not understand why it was that it appeared, in merely crossing the boundary, I had entered a completely fresh type of landscape. It was a wide green valley, where a small river sparkled, and vivid water birds darted over the rushes. The grass was thick and soft to my calves, the trees stood tall and shapely.

I was used to our farm, whose hundreds of acres of harsh eroded soil bore trees that had been cut for the mine furnaces and had grown thin and twisted, where the cattle had dragged the grass flat, leaving innumerable crisscrossing trails that deepened each season into gullies, under the force of the rains.

This country had been left untouched, save for prospectors whose picks had struck a few sparks from the surface of the rocks as they wandered by; and for migrant natives whose passing had left, perhaps, a charred patch on the trunk of a tree where their evening fire had nestled.

It was very silent: a hot morning with pigeons cooing throatily, the midday shadows lying dense and thick with clear yellow spaces of sunlight between and in all that wide green parklike valley, not a human soul but myself.

I was listening to the quick regular tapping of a woodpecker when slowly a chill feeling seemed to grow up from the small of my back to my shoulders, in a constricting spasm like a shudder, and at the roots of my hair a tingling sensation began and ran down over the surface of my flesh, leaving me goosefleshed and cold, though I was damp with sweat. Fever? I thought; then uneasily turned to look over my shoulder; and realized suddenly that this was fear. For all the years I had walked by myself over this country I had never known a moment's uneasiness; in the beginning because I had been supported by a gun and the dogs, then because I had learnt an easy friendliness for the Africans I might encounter.

I had read of this feeling, how the bigness and silence of Africa, under the ancient sun, grows dense and takes shape in the mind, till even the birds seem to call menacingly, and a deadly spirit comes out of the trees and the rocks. You move warily, as if your very passing disturbs something old and evil, something dark and big and angry that might suddenly rear and strike from behind. You look at groves of entwined trees, and picture the animals that might be lurking there; you look at the river running slowly, dropping from level to level through the vlei, spreading into pools where at night the bucks come to drink, and the crocodiles rise and drag them by their soft noses into underwater caves. Fear possessed me. I found I was turning round and round, because of that shapeless menace behind me that might reach out and take me; I kept glancing at the files of *kopjes* which, seen from a different angle, seemed to change with every step so that even known landmarks, like a big mountain that had sentinelled my world since I first became conscious of it, showed an unfamiliar sunlit valley among its foothills. I did not know where I was. I was lost. Panic seized me. I found I was spinning round and round, staring anxiously at this tree and that, peering up at the sun, which appeared to have moved into an eastern slant, shedding the sad yellow light of sunset. Hours must have passed! I looked at my watch and found that this state of meaningless terror had lasted perhaps ten minutes.

The point was that it was meaningless. I was not ten miles from home: I had only to take my way back along the valley to find myself at the fence; away among the foothills of the *kopjes* gleamed the roof of a neighbor's house, and a couple of hours' walking would reach it. This was the sort of fear that contracts the flesh of a dog at night and sets him howling at the full moon. It had nothing to do with what I thought or felt; and I was more disturbed by the fact that I could become its victim than of the physical sensation itself: I walked steadily on, quietened, in a divided mind, watching my own pricking nerves and apprehensive glances from side to side with a disgusted amusement. Deliberately I set myself to think of this village I was seeking, and what I should do when I entered it—if I could find it, which was doubtful, since I was walking aimlessly and it might be anywhere in the hundreds of thousands of acres of bush that stretched about me. With my mind on that village, I realized that a new sensation was added to the fear: loneliness. Now such a terror of isolation invaded me that I could hardly walk; and if it were not that I came over the crest of a small rise and saw a village below me, I should have turned and gone home. It was a cluster of thatched huts in a clearing among trees. There were neat patches of mealies and pumpkins and millet, and cattle grazed under some trees at a distance. Fowls scratched among the huts, dogs lay sleeping on the grass, and goats friezed a *kopje* that jutted up beyond a tributary of the river lying like an enclosing arm round the village.

As I came close I saw the huts were lovingly decorated with patterns of yellow and red and ochre mud on the walls; and the thatch was tied in place with plaits of straw.

This was not at all like our farm compound, a dirty and neglected place, a temporary home for migrants who had no roots in it.

And now I did not know what to do next. I called a small black boy, who was sitting on a lot playing a stringed gourd, quite naked except for the strings of blue beads round his neck, and said: "Tell the Chief I am here." The child stuck his thumb in his mouth and stared shyly back at me.

For minutes I shifted my feet on the edge of what seemed a deserted village, till at last the child scuttled off, and then some women came. They were draped in bright cloths, with brass glinting in their ears and on their arms. They also stared, silently; then turned to chatter among themselves.

I said again: "Can I see Chief Mshlanga?" I saw they caught the name; they did not understand what I wanted. I did not understand myself.

At last I walked through them and came past the huts and saw a clearing under a big shady tree, where a dozen old men sat cross-legged on the ground, talking. Chief Mshlanga was leaning back against the tree, holding a gourd in his hand, from which he had been drinking. When he saw me, not a muscle of his face moved, and I could see he was not pleased: perhaps he was afflicted with my own shyness, due to being unable to find the right forms of courtesy for the occasion. To meet me, on our own farm, was one thing, but I should not have come here. What had I expected? I could not join them socially: the thing was unheard of. Bad enough that I, a white girl, should be walking the veld alone as a white man might: and in this part of the bush where only Government officials had the right to move.

Again I stood, smiling foolishly, while behind me stood the groups of brightly clad, chattering women, their faces alert with curiosity and interest, and in front of me sat the old men, with old lined faces, their eyes guarded, aloof. It was a village of ancients and children and women. Even the two young men who kneeled beside the

Chief were not those I had seen with him previously: the young men were all away working on the white men's farms and mines, and the Chief must depend on relatives who were temporarily on holiday for his attendants.

"The small white Nkosikaas is far from home," remarked the old man at last.

"Yes," I agreed, "it is far." I wanted to say: "I have come to pay you a friendly visit, Chief Mshlanga." I could not say it. I might now be feeling an urgent helpless desire to get to know these men and women as people, to be accepted by them as a friend, but the truth was I had set out in a spirit of curiosity: I had wanted to see the village that one day our cook, the reserved and obedient young man who got drunk on Sundays, would rule over.

"The child of Nkosi Jordan is welcome," said Chief Mshlanga.

"Thank you," I said, and could think of nothing more to say. There was a silence, while the flies rose and began to buzz around my head; and the wind shook a little in the thick green tree that spread its branches over the old men.

"Good morning," I said at last. "I have to return now to my home."

"Morning, little Nkosikaas," said Chief Mshlanga.

I walked away from the indifferent village, over the rise past the staring amber-eyed goats, down through the tall stately trees into the great rich green valley where the river meandered and the pigeons cooed tales of plenty and the woodpecker tapped softly.

The fear had gone; the loneliness had set into stiff-necked stoicism; there was now a queer hostility in the landscape, a cold, hard, sullen indomitability that walked with me, as strong as a wall, as intangible as smoke; it seemed to say to me: you walk here as a destroyer. I went slowly homewards, with an empty heart: I had learned that if one cannot call a country to heel like a dog, neither can one dismiss the past with a smile in an easy gush of feeling, saying: I could not help it, I am also a victim.

I only saw Chief Mshlanga once again.

One night my father's big red land was trampled down by small sharp hooves, and it was discovered that the culprits were goats from Chief Mshlanga's kraal. This had happened once before, years ago.

My father confiscated all the goats. Then he

sent a message to the old Chief that if he wanted them he would have to pay for the damage.

He arrived at our house at the time of sunset one evening, looking very old and bent now, walking stiffly under his regally draped blanket, leaning on a big stick. My father sat himself down in his big chair below the steps of the house; the old man squatted carefully on the ground before him, flanked by his two young men.

The palaver was long and painful, because of the bad English of the young man who interpreted, and because my father could not speak dialect, but only kitchen kaffir.

From my father's point of view, at least two hundred pounds' worth of damage had been done to the crop. He knew he could not get the money from the old man. He felt he was entitled to keep the goats. As for the old Chief, he kept repeating angrily: "Twenty goats! My people cannot lose twenty goats! We are not rich, like the Nkosi Jordan, to lose twenty goats at once."

My father did not think of himself as rich, but rather as very poor. He spoke quickly and angrily in return, saying that the damage done meant a great deal to him, and that he was entitled to the goats.

At last it grew so heated that the cook, the

Chief's son, was called from the kitchen to be interpreter, and now my father spoke fluently in English, and our cook translated rapidly so that the old man could understand how very angry my father was. The young man spoke without emotion, in a mechanical way, his eyes lowered, but showing how he felt his position by a hostile uncomfortable set of the shoulders.

It was now in the late sunset, the sky a welter of colours, the birds singing their last songs, and the cattle, lowing peacefully, moving past us towards their sheds for the night. It was the hour when Africa is most beautiful; and here was this pathetic, ugly scene, doing no one any good.

At last my father stated finally: "I'm not going to argue about it. I am keeping the goats."

The old Chief flashed back in his own language: "That means that my people will go hungry when the dry season comes."

"Go to the police, then," said my father, and looked triumphant.

There was, of course, no more to be said.

The old man sat silent, his head bent, his hands dangling helplessly over his withered knees. Then he rose, the young men helping him, and he stood facing my father. He spoke once again, very stiffly; and turned away and went home to his village.

"What did he say?" asked my father of the young man, who laughed uncomfortably and would not meet his eyes.

"What did he say?" insisted my father.

Our cook stood straight and silent, his brows knotted together. Then he spoke, "My father says: All this land, this land you call yours, is his land, and belongs to our people."

Having made this statement, he walked off into the bush after his father, and we did not see him again.

Our next cook was a migrant from Nyasaland, with no expectations of greatness.

Next time the policeman came on his rounds he was told this story. He remarked: "That kraal has no right to be there; it should have been moved long ago. I don't know why no one has done anything about it. I'll have a chat with the Native Commissioner next week. I'm going over for tennis on Sunday, anyway."

Some time later we heard that Chief Mshlanga and his people had been moved two hundred miles east, to a proper Native Reserve; the Government land was going to be opened up for white settlement soon.

I went to see the village again, about a year afterwards. There was nothing there. Mounds of red mud, where the huts had been, had long swathes of rotting thatch over them, veined with the red galleries of the white ants. The pumpkin vines rioted everywhere, over the bushes, up the lower branches of trees so that the great golden balls rolled underfoot and dangled overhead: it was a festival of pumpkins. The bushes were crowding up, the new grass sprang vivid green.

The settler lucky enough to be allotted the lush warm valley (if he chose to cultivate this particular section) would find, suddenly, in the middle of a mealie field, the plants were growing fifteen feet tall, the weight of the cobs dragging at the stalks, and wonder what unsuspected vein of richness he had struck.

A Day in the Country

Dan Jacobson

We had spent the day on the farm, as we usually did every Sunday. Rather a dull day it had been, I remember, in April, too cold to go swimming in the river, and there had been nothing much else to do except sit in the car and watch my father as he helped the boys round up the cattle driven down from the veld, and then walk through them, stick in hand, prodding their sides, stopping to discuss at length what to do about the heifer who was going blind in one eye, or what a pity it was that this miserable beast should be in calf again when what it needed was a long rest. My father could spend hours like that, perfectly happy among the slow red cows and oxen, with the African herd boy who knew each head of cattle as an individual and respected it as such. And my father prodded, leaned against his stick, screwed

46

his face up against the sun, listened to the herd boy's comments, and twisted his ankle on one of the rocks that littered the piece of veld where the cattle were gathered.

When he ricked his ankle, my father had had enough. He got back into the car and we set off home, with the herd boy's children riding with us on the back bumper, as far as the gate. At the gate they climbed off and opened it for us; we passed through, they waved, and we waved back. Now there was just the thirty-mile run home, through Rietpan, bypassing Dors River, meeting the tarred road to take us to the Boer War Memorial—and so home. My brother was driving, my father and mother sat in front with him, and my sister and I were in the backseat. The first stretch of road was really bad, not a road at all, but a cart track across Rietpan Commonage, a piece of veld that had been grazed to complete nudity by the donkeys of the villagers. A few donkeys, a cow or two, one or two goats: those were generally the sole possessions of the Rietpan villagers, that and a mud-walled house and five irrigated acres. But though Rietpan was poor, it had its location, even poorer, where the black-skinned inhabitants of the village lived. They were conducting some sort of religious rite as we passed the location, and a man held up a cross of plaited twigs towards us. He was wearing a blue cowl on his head. The wind blew all their clothes in bright fluttering rags as they walked behind the leader. The sun shone bare upon them through the wind.

Inside the car it was dull and dusty, with the Sunday newspapers in a mess on the floor. My sister was knitting. We passed through Rietpan quickly, in a cloud of dust, with a greeting for Major le Roy on his front stoep and a pause to give way for someone's sheep. The road between Rietpan and Dors River was better, and my brother increased his speed.

My father looked up from the comic he was reading. He read it with an air of absolute puzzlement: "Who reads these things?" he asked. Then: "Oh, oh, oh, boy, slow down." He placed a hand on my brother's arm. There was a car standing in the middle of the road, and a group of people at the side of the road, looking down at something.

We thought it was an accident. It looked like an accident. We prepared ourselves for something horrible and warily our car crept up to the other, then drove past it and stopped.

"What is it?" my sister said shrilly.

"I don't know." We couldn't see. The other car was blocking our view of what the little group was seeing. Our car went forward a few feet. Dear God, it was an accident. The group stood over a little African child, a group of white men and women. A few Africans stood a little way off, looking at what was going on, and saying nothing. The white people were talking to one another. They seemed quite unmoved, almost lighthearted, but the black child lay still on the ground. I could see its spindly legs like winter branches of a tree, lying still on the ground.

"What is it?" my father called out through the window of the car, and as he did so, one of the white men stooped and picked the child up. The black legs kicked wildly, and a shriek went up from the child. I saw one of the Africans take a pace forward, then fall back. The group turned to their car, one man still carrying the child. And then I saw a strange thing. They were laughing, all of them were laughing. The child still screamed and kicked, and then writhed over in the man's arms, away from the motorcar, butting its head into the broad grey-shirted chest, as a child turns into its mother's arms for protection. We saw white face after face, all bared in smiles, and their laughter surrounded the thin screams of the child, until one could no longer believe that what one heard was truly a scream of fear.

"What is it?" my father called again. But no one took any notice. One of the men ran forward and opened the bonnet of the car. We heard him say in Afrikaans, "Come on, put him in," and the child screamed again, awfully.

But we knew now. It wasn't an accident, it was a game. I don't know whether we felt more relief or disgust. One of the grinning men saw us watching them, and still with his grin, he waved to us that we could go on. They didn't need our help; it wasn't an accident. None of us grinned back at him. I think he saw that we weren't amused at his game, for he looked away.

"For God's sake let's go."

"I've had enough of this."

My brother started the car. As we drove off I said, "What dirty swine." I looked through the back window of the car. They had put the child back on the road, one of the men was standing halfway in his car, the bonnet was down. Apparently the game was breaking up. We hoped that it was our condemnation that had broken it up. Yet there was the taste of guilt in each of our mouths that we had just looked our condemnation and not said anything to them, not made a protest in the name of humanity. But we were used to that sort of scene and that sort of guilt. Together they almost make up a way of life.

We had driven on only a short distance when with a roar of wind and a cloud of dust the car passed us. As it whipped past, one of the men in it leaned his head, half his body, out of the window, and shouted something at us. None of us heard what he was shouting, it was lost in the wind and the dust. All we saw was a white shirt and a white face and a pair of bright-red lips opening and closing grotesquely.

Now you don't shout insults at my father. My brother and I swore ineffectually at the billows of dust which followed their car, but my father, in a moment, was trembling with rage.

"Chase them," he shouted.

"Don't be mad," my brother said.

"Then stop the car."

"Why? What for?"

"I'll show you why. Stop the car." My brother didn't, so my father leaned over and switched off the ignition key.

My brother lost his temper as the car slowed

down and stopped. "All right, take your bloody car," he said, and got out and came in the back, slamming the door behind him.

"Michael, what are you going to do?" my mother asked.

My brother and I were both yelling at my father to leave it, cut it out, forget the whole business, and he was saying, "No one shouts at me like that. No one shouts at me like that," as we tore along the road. We could see the other car ahead of us, still raising dust. But we were catching up with it. Soon we were in the car's cloud of dust. Small stones struck against the windshield, and we could see very little through the grey murk.

"Michael, you're going to have an accident."

"I'm not going to have an accident."

"For God's sake, Dad, let's not have a scene."

"What do you mean let's not have a scene, when they shout at me like that?"

"You don't even know what he shouted."

"I know well enough what he shouted."

"What did he shout?"

"No one shouts at me like that."

We came to the crossroads of the main road to Lyndhurst and the Rietpan–Dors River road. The front car went towards Dors River, so we went that way too, still at a dangerously high speed.

"Michael, you're going to have an accident."

Dors River was about us. J. Wassenaar *Algemene Handelaar*/General Dealer. There was the station. The road passed J. Wassenaar and then turned round a corner, the hotel, the Savoy, with two petrol pumps in front of it. Then there was a house, another, a piece of veld, two more houses, and a last shop. In front of the last shop stood the black Dodge we had been chasing. The people were climbing out of it. One of them, the man in the white shirt, the one who had shouted, saw us coming and stood looking at us with his mouth open.

Again we drew level with the car. Inside our car, everyone with the exception of my father was dreading the scene that we knew was about to follow.

We stopped. My father said: "How dare you shout at me like that."

Now they were all out of their car. There were six of them, three men and three women. They stood at various points round their car, looking at us.

The young man in the grey shirt said, "What's the matter with you?" He was big and dirty, the one who had been carrying the child. He wore a broad-brimmed hat on the back of his head, and it made his face look round and flabby, under the circling rim of his hat. But he was big and strong, with enormous bare arms folded on his chest. I knew that if it did come to a fight he would be the one to give us the most trouble, and the one who would probably beat us at that. He walked over to our car, arms still folded, contemptuously, and said again: "What's the matter with you?"

But he was speaking English. Was that already a victory for us? He was speaking our language, we weren't speaking his. But he was big, much bigger than any of us as he stood at the driver's window of the car and said: "What's the matter with you?"

My father suddenly blazed out at him. "What sort of a person are you? First you torture a child that's done nothing to you, and then you scream at someone you're passing on the road. Well, let me tell you that I'm not a little Kaffir piccanin. You can't do what you like with me. I'll teach you manners before I'm finished with you."

The man said, "How?" He added: "You're too old." And it was true, pitifully true, my father was too old to fight him. He could have killed the old man.

This was the cue for my brother and myself. We climbed out of the car and walked round. The big man wheeled to face us. I saw his muscles tighten under the hair of his arms, and I knew that if we were to win this argument it wouldn't be by force. But we stared at each other as though we weren't frightened. He probably wasn't.

My father said: "You people make me sick. You've got no idea how to behave. But if you think you can go round bullying everybody like you bully that Kaffir child you're mistaken." He opened the door of the car as though to come out, and quickly the man darted at it, to slam it on him. With me a little way behind him my brother moved towards the man. My brother said: "No you don't." He was panting as he spoke, as though he had been running in a race.

Now, if there was to be a fight, it would be now. But there was no fight, and I did not understand why, as the old man, apparently the father of the two younger ones, came up and said, "You've got no right to talk like that about my people. We weren't doing anything to the piccanin." He gestured, almost appealingly.

We stared at him. He said again, "You've got no right to talk like that about my people"—and then I realized that our fear, the fear that we would be called "Bloody Jews," the fear which perhaps had kept our mouths closed when we had seen the piccanin being tortured—was his fear too. He, the Afrikaner who spoke English to us, felt that my father was sitting in his car and despising him for the race he belonged to, and judging him and his race by what we had seen on the road; and I realized, how happily, that the father did not want to be judged by that act, and did not want his son to fight us, for even if we should fight and his son should beat us, our original and damning judgement would remain, would even be confirmed. He didn't want to beat us, he wanted us to think well of his race, and how could he do that while the piccanin screamed with terror and kicked helplessly against his son's arms? He stayed his son's arm, and said, "It was only a bit of fun and you had no right to swear at us."

"Swear at you?" my father asked.

"Yes, swear at us," the other son said, coming up. I saw then why his lips were so red. It was lipstick on his mouth. It must have come from the lips of one of the girls who were leaning against the mudguards of the other car, watching the scene. Like his father, this son did not want to fight. He said, "We heard you swearing as you drove off."

"You were the one," my father said, interrupting him. "You were the one who leaned out of the car and shouted." My father looked at him.

He wiped his mouth with his hand. There was another smear of lipstick on his cheekbone. He said, "I shouted at you to mind your own business."

"But we said nothing to you. We didn't like what you were doing, but we didn't say anything to you."

"You said 'bloody swine.' "

"That's simply not true," my father said.

I said nothing.

"I heard you," the man repeated.

"You couldn't have heard it because no one said it."

And despite this foolish wrangling, the tension remained where it had been all along, where it had been when it had looked as though there was to be a physical fight. The unspoken words lay heavily on our tongues: *Dutchmen, Jews*. But they were never used. Racial tensions usually hasten fights, but this time they didn't, for they were too widely shared. Our fear was theirs: it was almost as though we cooperated with one another to keep the significance of the argument hidden, yet never for a moment forgot it. Had we not been Jews, we might have reproved them more strongly for what they did to the piccanin—for kinship in oppression, or fear of oppression, has two sides, one less noble than the other; and had they not been Afrikaners who feared that their reputation was one of brutality, uncouthness and oppression—all of which they had confirmed, they feared—they might simply have fought us off. But we were all prevented from fighting, and prevented from peace.

I remember the father saying, "Do you think we would have done anything to that piccanin? We aren't mad people. It was just a bit of fun among ourselves."

And the younger son, who did not want to fight, spoke earnestly to me. "You see, this little native child ran right across our car, in front of our car, and I had to brake like hell not to knock him over. So we thought we'll give him a lesson he'll remember. It's for his own good too, you know. He'll be a damn sight more careful now. He'll look what's going on before he runs across the road. Perhaps he'll live longer that way." Tentatively he smiled at me.

The father was saying, "You see that boy there, he goes to university. In Pretoria. Already he's in his second-year studies. A university student. Do you think that people like that, university students, gentlemen, educated people, are going to

do anything that they'll be ashamed of
afterwards? . . ."

I said, "You made a mistake. No one shouted
'bloody swine'." What I said was true, but it was
a lie too. In all that squalor it hardly mattered,
but I had to add: "But we didn't like what you
were doing."

"All right, then I shouldn't have shouted at
you from my car. But it was our business what we
were doing with that piccanin, especially as we
weren't going to hurt him. It was only a bit of
sport."

"Not a very nice sport," my mother called out.
We seemed to be winning all the way down the
line. The big son had moved away and was being
ignored by everybody. The other two continued
their laboured explanations, struggling for English
words to express themselves in. Once the father
veered towards an aggressive tone, and then, as
though remembering the faces in the car, closed
and hostile, with the struggling black body in his
son's arms, as guilty as blood, he became defensive
again.

So a sort of peace did come, and we got back
into the car. No one shook hands with anyone,
there had been no reconciliation to warrant that.
But no blows had been struck, and no one had

called anyone a bloody Dutchman or a bloody Jew, so everything was as well as could be expected. Better really, for us, because we still despised them. We despised that family: it is not our fault they misinterpreted it. And they should have known that we were as frightened of them as they were of us. We left them there, outside their whitewashed shop with the house behind it, that looked across the sand road to the railway line and the railway paddock where one chestnut horse was growing thin in transit between two lost farms.

It was a quiet journey home. Everyone was feeling depressed and beaten, though, as I have explained, the victory was ours. But we had all lost, so much, somewhere, farther back, along that dusty road.

Country Lovers

Nadine Gordimer

The farm children play together when they are small; but once the white children go away to school they soon don't play together anymore, even in the holidays. Although most of the black children get some sort of schooling, they drop every year farther behind the grades passed by the white children; the childish vocabulary, the child's exploration of the adventurous possibilities of dam, koppies, mealie lands, and veld—there comes a time when the white children have surpassed these with the vocabulary of boarding school and the possibilities of interschool sports matches and the kind of adventures seen at the cinema. This usefully coincides with the age of twelve or thirteen; so that by the time early adolescence is reached, the black children are making, along with the bodily changes common to all, an easy transition to adult forms of address, beginning to call their old playmates *missus* and *baasie*—little master.

The trouble was Paulus Eysendyck did not seem to realize that Thebedi was now simply one of the crowd of farm children down at the kraal, recognizable in his sisters' old clothes. The first Christmas holidays after he had gone to boarding school he brought home for Thebedi a painted box he had made in his woodwork class. He had to give it to her secretly because he had nothing for the other children at the kraal. And she gave him, before he went back to school, a bracelet she had made of thin brass wire and the grey-and-white beans of the castor-oil crop his father cultivated. (When they used to play together, she was the one who had taught Paulus how to make clay oxen for their toy spans.) There was a craze, even in the *platteland* towns like the one where he was at school, for boys to wear elephant-hair and other bracelets beside their watch straps; his was admired, friends asked him to get similar ones for them. He said the natives made them on his father's farm and he would try.

When he was fifteen, six feet tall, and tramping round at school dances with the girls from the "sister" school in the same town; when he had learnt how to tease and flirt and fondle quite intimately these girls who were the daughters of prosperous farmers like his father; when he had even met one who, at a wedding he had attended with his parents on a nearby farm, had let him do with her in a locked storeroom what people did when they made love—when he was as far from his childhood as all this, he still brought home from a shop in town a red plastic belt and gilt hoop earrings for the black girl, Thebedi. She told her father the missus had given these to her as a reward for some work she had done—it was true she sometimes was called to help out in the farmhouse. She told the girls in the kraal that she had a sweetheart nobody knew about, far away, away on another farm, and they giggled, and teased, and admired her. There was a boy in the kraal called Njabulo who said he wished he could have bought her a belt and earrings.

When the farmer's son was home for the holidays she wandered far from the kraal and her companions. He went for walks alone. They had not arranged this; it was an urge each followed independently. He knew it was she, from a long way off. She knew that his dog would not bark at her. Down at the dried-up riverbed where five or six years ago the children had caught a leguaan one great day—a creature that combined ideally the size and ferocious aspect of the crocodile with the harmlessness of the lizard—they squatted side by side on the earth bank. He told her traveller's tales: about school, about the punishments at school, particularly, exaggerating both their nature and his indifference to them. He told her about the town of Middleburg, which she had never seen. She had nothing to tell but she prompted with many questions, like any good listener. While he talked he twisted and tugged at the roots of white stinkwood and Cape willow trees that looped out of the eroded earth around them. It had always been a good spot for children's games, down there hidden by the mesh of old, ant-eaten trees held in place by vigorous ones, wild asparagus bushing up between the trunks, and here and there prickly-pear cactus sunken-skinned and bristly, like an old man's face, keeping alive sapless until the next rainy season. She punctured the dry hide of a prickly-pear again and again with a sharp stick while she listened. She laughed a lot at what he told her, sometimes dropping her face on her knees, sharing amusement with the cool shady earth beneath her bare feet. She put on her pair of shoes—white sandals, thickly Blancoed against the farm dust—when he was on the farm, but these were taken off and laid aside, at the riverbed.

One summer afternoon when there was water flowing there and it was very hot she waded in as they used to do when they were children, her dress bunched modestly and tucked into the legs of her pants. The schoolgirls he went swimming with at dams or pools on neighbouring farms wore bikinis but the sight of their dazzling bellies and thighs in the sunlight had never made him feel what he felt now, when the girl came up the bank and sat beside him, the drops of water beading off her dark legs the only points of light in the earth-smelling, deep shade. They were not afraid of one another, they had known one another always; he did with her what he had done that time in the storeroom at the wedding, and this time it was so lovely, so lovely, he was surprised . . . and she was surprised by it, too—he could see in her dark face that was part of the shade, with her big dark eyes, shiny as soft water, watching him attentively: as she had when they used to huddle over their teams of mud oxen, as she had when he told her about detention weekends at school.

They went to the riverbed often through those summer holidays. They met just before the light went, as it does quite quickly, and each returned home with the dark—she to her mother's hut, he to the farmhouse—in time for the evening meal. He did not tell her about school or town anymore. She did not ask questions any longer. He told her, each time, when they would meet again. Once or twice it was very early in the morning; the lowing of the cows being driven to graze came to them where they lay, dividing them with unspoken recognition of the sound read in their two pairs of eyes, opening so close to each other.

He was a popular boy at school. He was in the second, then the first soccer team. The head girl of the "sister" school was said to have a crush on him; he didn't particularly like her, but there was a pretty blonde who put up her long hair into a kind of doughnut with a black ribbon round it, whom he took to see films when the schoolboys and girls had a free Saturday afternoon. He had been driving tractors and other farm vehicles since he was ten years old, and as soon as he was eighteen he got a driver's licence and in the holidays, this last year of his school life, he took neighbours' daughters to dances and to the drive-in cinema that had just opened twenty kilometres from the farm. His sisters were married, by then; his parents often left him in charge of the farm over the weekend while they visited the young wives and grandchildren.

When Thebedi saw the farmer and his wife drive away on a Saturday afternoon, the boot of their Mercedes filled with fresh-killed poultry and vegetables from the garden that it was part of her father's work to tend, she knew that she must come not to the riverbed but up to the house. The house was an old one, thick-walled, dark against the heat. The kitchen was its lively thoroughfare, with servants, food supplies, begging cats and dogs, pots boiling over, washing being damped for ironing, and the big deep freeze the missus had ordered from town, bearing a crocheted mat and a vase of plastic irises. But the dining room with the bulging-legged heavy table was shut up in its rich, old smell of soup and tomato sauce. The sitting-room curtains were drawn and the T.V. set silent. The door of the parents' bedroom was locked and the empty rooms where the girls had slept had sheets of plastic spread over the beds. It was in one of these that she and the farmer's son stayed together whole nights—almost: she had to get away before the house servants, who knew her, came in at dawn. There was a risk someone would discover her or traces of her presence if he took her to his own bedroom, although she had looked into it many times when she was helping out in the house and knew well, there, the row of silver cups he had won at school.

When she was eighteen and the farmer's son nineteen and working with his father on the farm before entering a veterinary college, the young man Njabulo asked her father for her. Njabulo's parents met with hers and the money he was to pay in place of the cows it is customary to give a prospective bride's parents was settled upon. He had no cows to offer; he was a labourer on the Eysendyck farm, like her father. A bright youngster; old Eysendyck had taught him bricklaying and was using him for odd jobs in construction, around the place. She did not tell the farmer's son that her parents had arranged for her to marry. She did not tell him, either, before he left for his first term at the veterinary college, that she thought she was going to have a baby. Two months after her marriage to Njabulo, she gave birth to a daughter. There was no disgrace in that; among her people it is customary for a young man to make sure, before marriage, that the chosen girl is not barren, and Njabulo had made love to her then. But the infant was very light and did not quickly grow darker as most African babies do. Already at birth there was on its head a quantity of straight, fine floss, like that which carries the seeds of certain weeds in the veld. The unfocused eyes it opened were grey flecked with yellow. Njabulo was the matte, opaque coffeegrounds colour that has always been called black; the colour of Thebedi's legs on which beaded water looked oyster-shell blue, the same colour as Thebedi's face, where the black eyes, with their interested gaze and clear whites, were so dominant.

Njabulo made no complaint. Out of his farm labourer's earnings he bought from the Indian store a cellophane-windowed pack containing a pink plastic bath, six napkins, a card of safety pins, a knitted jacket, cap and bootees, a dress, and a tin of Johnson's Baby Powder, for Thebedi's baby.

When it was two weeks old Paulus Eysendyck arrived home from the veterinary college for the holidays. He drank a glass of fresh, still-warm milk in the childhood familiarity of his mother's kitchen and heard her discussing with the old house servant where they could get a reliable substitute to help out now that the girl Thebedi had had a baby. For the first time since he was a small boy he came right into the kraal. It was eleven o'clock in the morning. The men were at work in the lands. He looked about him, urgently; the women turned away, each not wanting to be the one approached to point out where Thebedi lived. Thebedi appeared, coming slowly from the hut Njabulo had built in white man's style, with a tin chimney, and a proper window with glass panes set in straight as walls made of unfired bricks would allow. She greeted him with hands brought together and a token movement representing the respectful bob with which she was accustomed to acknowledge she was in the presence of his father or mother. He lowered his head under the doorway of her home and went in. He said, "I want to see. Show me."

She had taken the bundle off her back before she came out into the light to face him. She moved between the iron bedstead made up with Njabulo's checked blankets and the small wooden table where the pink plastic bath stood among food and kitchen pots, and picked up the bundle from the snugly blanketed grocer's box where it lay. The infant was asleep; she revealed the closed, pale, plump tiny face, with a bubble of spit at the corner of the mouth, the spidery pink hands stirring. She took off the woollen cap and the straight fine hair flew up after it in static electricity, showing gilded strands here and there. He said nothing. She was watching him as she had done when they were little, and the gang of children had trodden down a crop in their games or transgressed in some other way for which he, as the farmer's son, the white one among them, must intercede with the farmer. She disturbed the sleeping face by scratching or tickling gently at a cheek with one finger, and slowly the eyes opened, saw nothing, were still asleep, and then, awake, no longer narrowed, looked out at them, grey with yellowish flecks, his own hazel eyes.

He struggled for a moment with a grimace of tears, anger and self-pity. She could not put out her hand to him. He said, "You haven't been near the house with it?"

She shook her head.

"Never?"

Again she shook her head.

"Don't take it out. Stay inside. Can't you take it away somewhere? You must give it to some-one—"

She moved to the door with him.

He said, "I'll see what I will do. I don't know." And then he said: "I feel like killing myself."

Her eyes began to glow, to thicken with tears.

For a moment there was the feeling between them that used to come when they were alone down at the riverbed.

He walked out.

Two days later, when his mother and father had left the farm for the day, he appeared again. The women were away on the lands, weeding, as they were employed to do as casual labour in summer; only the very old remained, propped up on the ground outside the huts in the flies and the sun. Thebedi did not ask him in. The child had not been well; it had diarrhoea. He asked where its food was. She said, "The milk comes from me." He went into Njabulo's house, where the child lay; she did not follow but stayed outside the door and watched without seeing an old crone who had lost her mind, talking to herself, talking to the fowls who ignored her.

She thought she heard small grunts from the hut, the kind of infant grunt that indicates a full stomach, a deep sleep. After a time, long or short she did not know, he came out and walked away with plodding stride (his father's gait) out of sight, towards his father's house.

The baby was not fed during the night and although she kept telling Njabulo it was sleeping, he saw for himself in the morning that it was dead. He comforted her with words and caresses. She did not cry but simply sat, staring at the door. Her hands were cold as dead chickens' feet to his touch.

Njabulo buried the little baby where farm workers were buried, in the place in the veld the farmer had given them. Some of the mounds had been left to weather away unmarked, others were covered with stones and a few had fallen wooden crosses. He was going to make a cross but before it was finished the police came and dug up the grave and took away the dead baby: someone— one of the other labourers? their women?—had reported that the baby was almost white, that, strong and healthy, it had died suddenly after a visit by the farmer's son. Pathological tests on the infant corpse showed intestinal damage not always consistent with death by natural causes.

Thebedi went for the first time to the country town where Paulus had been to school, to give evidence at the preparatory examination into the charge of murder brought against him. She cried hysterically in the witness box, saying yes, yes (the gilt hoop earrings swung in her ears), she saw the accused pouring liquid into the baby's mouth. She said he had threatened to shoot her if she told anyone.

More than a year went by before, in that same town, the case was brought to trial. She came to Court with a newborn baby on her back. She wore gilt hoop earrings; she was calm; she said she had not seen what the white man did in the house.

Paulus Eysendyck said he had visited the hut but had not poisoned the child.

The Defence did not contest that there had been a love relationship between the accused and the girl, or that intercourse had taken place, but submitted there was no proof that the child was the accused's.

The judge told the accused there was strong suspicion against him but not enough proof that he had committed the crime. The Court could not accept the girl's evidence because it was clear she had committed perjury either at this trial or at the preparatory examination. There was the suggestion in the mind of the Court that she might be an accomplice in the crime; but, again, insufficient proof.

The judge commended the honourable behaviour of the husband (sitting in court in a brown-and-yellow-quartered golf cap bought for Sundays) who had not rejected his wife and had "even provided clothes for the unfortunate infant out of his slender means."

The verdict on the accused was "not guilty."

The young white man refused to accept the congratulations of press and public and left the Court with his mother's raincoat shielding his face from photographers. His father said to the press, "I will try and carry on as best I can to hold up my head in the district."

Interviewed by the Sunday papers, who spelled her name in a variety of ways, the black girl, speaking in her own language, was quoted beneath her photograph: "It was a thing of our childhood, we don't see each other anymore."

When the Train Comes

Zoë Wicomb

I am not the kind of girl whom boys look at. I have known this for a long time, but I still lower my head in public and peep through my lashes. Their eyes leap over me, a mere obstacle in a line of vision. I should be pleased; boys can use their eyes shamelessly to undress a girl. That is what Sarie says. Sarie's hand automatically flutters to her throat to button up her orlon cardigan when boys talk to her. I have tried that, have fumbled with buttons and suffered their perplexed looks or reddened at the question, "Are you cold?"

I know that it is the act of guiding the buttons through their resistant holes that guides the eyes to Sarie's breasts.

Today I think that I would welcome any eyes that care to confirm my new ready-made polyester dress. Choosing has not brought an end to doubt.

The white, grey and black stripes run vertically, and from the generous hem I have cut a strip to replace the treacherous horizontal belt. I am not wearing a cardigan, even though it is unusually cool for January, a mere eighty degrees. I have looked once or twice at the clump of boys standing with a huge radio out of which the music winds mercurial through the rise and fall of distant voices. There is no music in our house. Father says it is distracting. We stand uneasily on the platform. The train is late or perhaps we are early. Pa stands with his back to the boys who have greeted him deferentially. His broad shoulders block my view but I can hear their voices flashing like the village lights on Republic Day. The boys do not look at me and I know why. I am fat. My breasts are fat and, in spite of my uplift bra, flat as a vetkoek.

There is a lump in my throat which I cannot account for. I do of course cry from time to time about being fat, but this lump will not be dislodged by tears. I am pleased that Pa does not say much. I watch him take a string out of his pocket and wind it nervously around his index finger. Round and round from the base until the finger is encased in a perfect bandage. The last is a loop that fits the tip of his finger tightly; the ends are tied in an almost invisible knot. He hopes to hold my attention with this game. Will this be followed by cat's cradle with my hands foolishly stretched out, waiting to receive? I smart at his attempts to shield me from the boys; they are quite unnecessary.

Pa knows nothing of young people. On the morning of my fourteenth birthday he quoted from <u>Genesis III</u> . . . <u>in pain you shall bring forth children</u>. I had been menstruating for some time and so knew what he wanted to say. He said, "You must fetch a bucket of water in the evenings and wash the rags at night . . . have them ready for the next month . . . always be prepared . . . it does not always come on time. Your mother was never regular . . . the ways of the Lord . . ." and he shuffled off with the bicycle tire he was pretending to repair.

"But they sell things now in chemists' shops, towels you can throw away," I called after him.

"Yes"—he looked dubiously at the distant blue hills—"perhaps you could have some for emergencies. Always be prepared," and lowering his eyes once again blurted, "And don't play with boys now that you're a young lady, it's dangerous."

I have never played with boys. There were none to play with when we lived on the farm. I do not know why. The memory, of a little boy boring a big toe into the sand, surfaces. He is staring enviously at the little house I have carved into the sandbank. There are shelves on which my pots gleam and my one-legged Peggy sleeps on her bank of clay. In my house I am free to do anything, even invite the boy to play. I am proud of the sardine can in which two clay loaves bake in the sun. For my new china teapot I have built a stone shrine where its posy of pink roses remains forever fresh. I am still smiling at the boy as he deftly pulls a curious hose from the leg of his khaki shorts and, with one eye shut, aims an arc of yellow pee into the teapot. I do not remember the teapot ever having a lid.

There is a lump in my throat I cannot account for. I sometimes cry about being fat, of course, especially after dinner when the zip of my skirt sinks its teeth into my flesh. Then it is reasonable to cry. But I have after all stood on this platform countless times on the last day of the school holidays. Sarie and I, with Pa and Mr. Botha waving and shouting into the clouds of steam, Work Hard or Be Good. Here, under the black and white arms of the station sign, where succulents spent and shrivelled in autumn grow once again plump in winter before they burst into shocking spring flower. So that Pa would say, "The quarters slip by so quickly, soon the sun will be on Cancer and you'll be home again." Or, "When the summer train brings you back with your First Class Junior Certificate, the aloe will just be in flower." And so the four school quarters clicked by under the Kliprand station sign where the jewelled eyes of the ice plant wink in the sun all year round.

The very first lump in my throat he melted with a fervent whisper, "You must, Friedatjie, you must. There is no high school for us here and you don't want to be a servant. How would you like to peg out the madam's washing and hear the train you once refused to go on rumble by?" Then he slipped a bag of raisins into my hand. A terrifying image of a madam's menstrual rags that I have to wash swirls liquid red through my mind. I am grateful to be going hundreds of miles away from home; there is so much to be grateful for. One day I will drive a white car.

Pa takes a stick of biltong out of his pocket and the brine in my eyes retreats. I have no control over the glands under my tongue as they anticipate the salt. His pocketknife lifts off the seasoned and puckered surface and leaves a slab of marbled meat, dry and mirror smooth so that I long to rest my lips on it. Instead my teeth sink into the biltong and I am consoled. I eat <u>everything</u> he offers.

We have always started our day with mealie porridge. That is what miners eat twice a day, and they lift chunks of gypsum clean out of the earth. Father's eyes flash a red light over the breakfast table: "Don't leave anything on your plate. You must grow up to be big and strong. We are not paupers with nothing to eat. Your mother was thin and sickly, didn't eat enough. You don't want cheekbones that jut out like a Hottentot's. Fill them out until they're shiny and plump as pumpkins." The habit of obedience is fed daily with second helpings of mealie porridge. He does not know that I have long since come to despise my size. I would like to be a pumpkin stored on the flat roof and draw in whole beams of autumn's sunlight so that, <u>bleached</u> and hardened, I could call upon the secret of my <u>glowing orange flesh.</u>

A wolf whistle from one of the boys. I turn to look and I know it will upset Pa. Two girls in identical flared skirts arrive with their own radio blaring Boeremusiek. They nod at us and stand close by, perhaps seeking protection from the boys. I hope that Pa will not speak to me loudly in English. I will avoid calling him Father for they will surely snigger under cover of the whining

concertina. They must know that for us this is no
ordinary day. But we all remain silent and I am
inexplicably ashamed. What do people say about
us? Until recently I believed that I was envied;
that is, not counting my appearance.

The boys beckon and the girls turn up their
radio. One of them calls loudly, "Turn off that
Boere-shit and come and listen to decent American music." I wince. The girls do as they are
told, their act of resistance deflated. [Pa casts an
anxious glance at the white policeman pacing the
actual platform, the paved white section. I take
out a paper handkerchief and wipe the dust from
my polished shoes, a futile act since this unpaved
strip, for which I have no word other than the
inaccurate platform, is all dust.] But it gives me
the chance to peer at the group of young people
through my lowered lashes.

The boys vie for their attention. They have
taken the radio and pass it round so that the red
skirts flare and swoop, the torsos in T-shirts arch
and taper into long arms reaching to recover their
radio. Their ankles swivel on the slender stems
of high heels. Their feet are covered in dust. One
of the arms adjusts a chiffon headscarf that threat-
ens to slip off, and a pimply boy crows at his

[handwritten margin notes: white section is paved and painted white, colors are in the dirt; colored section is dust, dirt]

advantage. He whips the scarf from her head and the tinkling laughter switches into a whine.

"Give it back. . . . You have no right. . . . It's mine and I want it back. . . . Please, oh please."

Her arm is raised protectively over her head, the hand flattened on her hair.

"No point in holding your head now," he teases. "I've got it, going to try it on myself."

Her voice spun thin on threads of tears, abject as she begs. So that her friend consoles, "It doesn't matter, you've got plenty of those. Show them you don't care." A reproachful look but the friend continues, "Really, it doesn't matter, your hair looks nice enough. I've told you before. Let him do what he wants with it, stuff it up his arse."

But the girl screams, "Leave me alone," and beats away the hand reaching out to console. Another taller boy takes the scarf and twirls it in the air. "You want your doekie? What do you want it for hey, come on tell us, what do you want it for? What do you want to cover up?"

His tone silences the others and his face tightens as he swings the scarf slowly, deliberately. She claws at his arm with rage while her face is buried in the other crooked arm. A little gust of wind settles the matter, whips it out of his hand and leaves it spread-eagled against the eucalyptus tree where its red pattern licks the bark like flames.

I cannot hear their words. But far from being penitent, the tall boy silences the bareheaded girl with angry shaking of the head and wagging of the finger. He runs his hand through an exuberant bush of fuzzy hair and my hand involuntarily flies to my own. I check my preparations: the wet hair wrapped over large rollers to separate the strands, dried then swirled around my head, secured overnight with a nylon stocking, dressed with Vaseline to keep the strands smooth and straight and then pulled back tightly to stem any remaining tendency to curl. Father likes it pulled back. He says it is a mark of honesty to have the forehead and ears exposed. He must be thinking of Mother, whose hair was straight and trouble free. I would not allow some unkempt youth to comment on my hair.

The tall boy with wild hair turns to look at us. I think that they are talking about me. I feel my body swelling out of the dress rent into vertical strips that fall to my feet. The wind will surely lift off my hair like a wig and flatten it, a sheet of glossy dead bird, on the eucalyptus tree.

[handwritten marginalia: hair is bushy and frizzy]

[handwritten marginalia: What is so much to make her hair straight? goes through, makes her hair straight]

The bareheaded girl seems to have recovered; she holds her head reasonably high.

I break the silence. "Why should that boy look at us so insolently?" Pa looks surprised and hurt. "Don't be silly. You couldn't possibly tell from this distance." But his mouth puckers and he starts an irritating tuneless whistle.

On the white platform the policeman is still pacing. He is there because of the Blacks who congregate at the station twice a week to see the Springbok train on its way to Cape Town. I wonder whether he knows our news. Perhaps their servants, bending over washtubs, ease their shoulders to give the gossip from Wesblok to madams limp with heat and boredom. But I dismiss the idea and turn to the boys who certainly know that I am going to St. Mary's today. All week the grown-ups have leaned over the fence and sighed, Ja, ja, in admiration, and winked at Pa: a clever chap, old Shenton, keeps up with the Boers all right. And to me, "You show them, Frieda, what we can do." I nodded shyly. Now I look at my hands, at the irrepressible cuticles, the stubby splayed fingernails that will never taper. This is all I have to show, betraying generations of servants.

I am tired and I move back a few steps to sit on the suitcases. But Father leaps to their defence. "Not on the cases, Frieda. They'll never take your weight." I hate the shiny suitcases. As if we had not gone to enough expense, he insisted on new imitation-leather bags and claimed that people judge by appearances. I miss my old scuffed bag and slowly, as if the notion has to travel through folds of fat, I realize that I miss Sarie and the lump in my throat hardens.

Sarie and I have travelled all these journeys together. Grief gave way to excitement as soon as we boarded the train. Huddled together on the cracked green seat, we argued about who would sleep on the top bunk. And in winter when the nights grew cold we folded into a single S on the lower bunk. As we tossed through the night in our magic coupé, our fathers faded and we were free. Now Sarie stands in the starched white uniform of a student nurse, the Junior Certificate framed in her father's room. She will not come to wave me good-bye.

Sarie and I swore our friendship on the very first day at school. We twiddled our stiff plaits in boredom; the *First Sunnyside Reader* had been read to us at home. And Jos. Within a week Jos had mastered the reader and joined us. The three of us hand in hand, a formidable string of laughing girls tugging this way and that, sneering at the Sunnyside adventures of Rover, Jane and John. I had no idea that I was fat. Jos looped my braids over her beautiful hands and said that I was pretty, that my braids were a string of sausages.

Jos was bold and clever. Like a whirlwind she spirited away the tedium of exhausted games and invented new rules. We waited for her to take command. Then she slipped her hand under a doekie of dyed flourbags and scratched her head. Her ear peeped out, a faded yellow-brown yearning for the sun. Under a star-crammed sky Jos had boldly stood for hours, peering through a crack in the shutter to watch their fifth baby being born. Only once had she looked away in agony and then the Three Kings in the eastern sky swiftly swopped places in the manner of musical chairs. She told us all, and with an oath invented by Jos we swore that we would never have babies. Jos knew everything that grown-ups thought should be kept from us. Father said, "A cheeky child, too big for her boots, she'll land in a madam's kitchen all right." But there was no need to separate us. Jos left school when she turned nine and her family moved to the village where her father had found a job at the garage. He had injured his back at the mine. Jos said they were going to have a car; that she would win one of those competitions, easy they were, you only had to make up a slogan.

Then there was our move. Pa wrote letters for the whole community, bit his nails when he thought I was not looking and wandered the veld for hours. When the official letter came the cooped-up words tumbled out helter-skelter in his longest monologue.

"In rows in the village, that's where we'll have to go, all boxed in with no room to stretch the legs. All my life I've lived in the open with only God to keep an eye on me, what do I want with the eyes of neighbours nudging and jostling in cramped streets? How will the wind get into those backyards to sweep away the smell of too many people? Where will I grow things? A watermelon, a pumpkin need room to spread, and a turkey wants a swept yard, the markings of a grass broom on which to boast the pattern of his wingmarks. What shall we do, Frieda? What will become of us?" And then, calmly, "Well, there's nothing to be done. We'll go to Wesblok, we'll put up our curtains and play with the electric lights and find a corner for the cat, but it won't be our home. I'm not clever old Shenton for nothing, not a wasted drop of Scots blood in me. Within five years we'll have enough to buy a little place. Just a little raw brick house and somewhere to tether a goat and keep a few chickens. Who needs a water lavatory in the veld?"

The voice brightened into fantasy. "If it were near a river we could have a pond for ducks or geese. In the Swarteberg my pa always had geese. Couldn't get to sleep for months here in Namaqualand without the squawking of geese. And ostriches. There's nothing like ostrich biltong studded with coriander seeds." Then he slowed down. "Ag man, we won't be allowed land by the river, but nevermind hey. We'll show them, Frieda, we will. You'll go to high school next year and board with Aunt Nettie. We've saved enough for that. Brains are for making money and when you come home with your Senior Certificate, you won't come back to a pack of Hottentots crouching in straight lines on the edge of the village. Oh no, my girl, you won't." And he whipped out a stick of beef biltong and with the knife shaved off wafer-thin slices that curled with pleasure in our palms.

We packed our things humming. I did not really understand what he was fussing about. The Coloured location did not seem so terrible. Electric lights meant no more oil lamps to clean and there was water from a tap at the end of each street. And there would be boys. But the children ran after me calling, "Fatty fatty vetkoek." Young children too. Sarie took me firmly by the arm and said that it wasn't true, that they were jealous of my long hair. I believed her and swung my stiff pigtails haughtily. Until I grew breasts and found that the children were right.

Now Sarie will be by the side of the sick and infirm, leaning over high hospital beds, soothing and reassuring. Sarie in a dazzling white uniform, her little waist clinched by the broad blue belt.

If Sarie were here I could be sure of climbing the two steel steps onto the train.

The tall boy is now pacing the platform in unmistakable imitation of the policeman. His face is the stern mask of someone who does not take his duties lightly. His friends are squatting on their haunches, talking earnestly. One of them illustrates a point with the aid of a stick with which he writes or draws in the sand. The girls have retreated and lean against the eucalyptus tree, bright as stars against the grey of the trunk. Twelve feet apart the two radios stand face to face, quarrelling quietly. Only the female voices rise now and again in bitter laughter above the machines.

Father says that he must find the stationmaster

to enquire why the train has not come. "Come with me," he commands. I find the courage to pretend that it is a question but I flush with the effort.

"No, I'm tired, I'll wait here." And he goes. It is true that I am tired. I do not on the whole have much energy and I am always out of breath. I have often consoled myself with an early death, certainly before I become an old maid. Alone with my suitcases I face the futility of that notion. I am free to abandon it since I am an old maid now, today, days after my fifteenth birthday. I do not in any case think that my spirit, weightless and energetic like smoke from green wood, will soar to heaven.

I think of Pa's defeated shoulders as he turned to go and I wonder whether I ought to run after him. But the thought of running exhausts me. I recoil again at the energy with which he had burst into the garden only weeks ago, holding aloft *Die Burger* with both hands, shouting, "Frieda, Frieda, we'll do it. It's all ours, the whole world's ours."

It was a short report on how a Coloured deacon had won his case against the Anglican Church so that the prestigious St. Mary's School was now open to nonwhites. The article ended sourly, calling it an empty and subversive gesture, and warning the deacon's daughters that it would be no bed of roses.

"You'll have the best, the very best education." His voice is hoarse with excitement.

"It will cost hundreds of rand per year."

"Nonsense, you finish this year at Malmesbury and then there'll be only the two years of Matric left to pay for. Really, it's a blessing that you have only two years left."

"Where will you find the money?" I say soberly.

"The nest egg of course, stupid child. You can't go to a white school if you're so stupid. Shenton has enough money to give his only daughter the best education in the world."

I hesitate before asking, "But what about the farm?" He has not come to like the Wesblok. The present he wraps in a protective gauze of dreams; his eyes have grown misty with focusing far ahead on the unrealized farm.

A muscle twitches in his face before he beams. "A man could live anywhere, burrow a hole like a rabbit in order to make use of an opportunity like this." He seizes the opportunity for a lecture. "Ignorance, laziness and tobacco have been the downfall of our people. It is our duty to God to better ourselves, to use our brains, our talents, not to place our lamps under bushels. No, we'll do it. We must be prepared to make sacrifices to meet such a generous offer."

His eyes race along the perimeter of the garden wall; then he rushes indoors, muttering about idling like flies in the sun, and sets about writing to St. Mary's in Cape Town.

I read novels and kept in the shade all summer. The crunch of biscuits between my teeth was the rumble of distant thunder. Pimples raged on my chin, which led me to Madame Rose's Preparation by mail order. That at least has fulfilled its promise.

I was surprised when Sarie wept with joy or envy, so that the tears spurted from my own eyes onto the pages of *Ritchie's First Steps in Latin*. (Father said that they pray in Latin and that I ought to know what I am praying for.) At night a hole crept into my stomach, gnawing like a hungry mouse, and I fed it with Latin declensions and Eetsumor biscuits. Sarie said that I might meet white boys and for the moment, fortified by conjugations of *Amo*, I saw the eyes of Anglican boys, remote princes leaning from their carriages, penetrate the pumpkin-yellow of my flesh.

Today I see a solid stone wall where I stand in watery autumn light waiting for a bell to ring. The Cape southeaster tosses high the blond pigtails and silvery laughter of girls walking by. They do not see me. Will I spend the dinner breaks hiding in lavatories?

I wish I could make this day more joyful for Pa but I do not know how. It is no good running after him now. It is too late.

The tall boy has imperceptibly extended his marching ground. Does he want to get closer to the policeman or is he taking advantage of Father's absence? I watch his feet, up, down, and the crunch of his soles on the sand explodes in my ears. Closer, and a thrilling thought shoots through the length of my body. He may be looking at me longingly, probing; but I cannot bring my eyes to travel up, along his unpressed trousers. The black boots of the policeman catch my eye. He will not be imitated. His heavy legs are tree trunks rooted in the asphalt. His hand rests on the bulge of his holster. I can no longer resist the crunch of the boy's soles as they return. I look up. He clicks his heels and halts. His eyes are narrowed with unmistakable contempt. He greets me in precise mocking English. A soundless shriek for Pa escapes my lips and I note the policeman resuming his march before I reply. The boy's voice is angry and I wonder what aspect of my dress offends him.

"You are waiting for the Cape Town train?" he asks unnecessarily. I nod.

"You start at the white school tomorrow?" A hole yawns in my stomach and I long for a biscuit. I will not reply.

"There are people who bury dynamite between the rails and watch whole carriages of white people shoot into the air. Like opening the door of a birdcage. Phsssh!" His long thin arms describe the spray of birdflight. "Perhaps that is why your train has not come."

I know he is lying. I would like to hurl myself at him, stab at his eyes with my blunt nails, kick at his ankles until they snap. But I clasp my hands together piously and hold, hold the tears that threaten.

"Your prayer is answered. Look, here's Fa-ath-errr," and on the held note he clicks his heels and turns smartly to march off towards his friends.

Father is smiling. "She's on her way, should be here any second now." I take his arm and my hand slips into his jacket pocket, where I trace with my finger the withered potato he wears for relief of rheumatism.

"No more biltong, girlie," he laughs. The hole in my stomach grows dangerously.

The white platform is now bustling with people.

Porters pile suitcases onto their trolleys while men fish in their pockets for sixpence tips. A Black girl staggers onto the white platform with a suitcase in each hand. Her madam ambles amiably alongside her to keep up with the faltering gait. She chatters without visible encouragement and, stooping, takes one of the bags from the girl, who clearly cannot manage. The girl is big boned with strong shapely arms and calves. What can the suitcase contain to make her stagger so? Her starched apron sags below the waist and the crisp servant's cap is askew. When they stop at the far end of the platform she slips a hand under the edge of the white cap to scratch. Briefly she tugs at the tip of her yellow-brown earlobe. My chest tightens. I turn to look the other way.

Our ears prick at a rumbling in the distance which sends as scout a thin squeal along the rails. A glass dome of terror settles over my head so that the chatter about me recedes and I gulp for air. But I do not faint. The train lumbers to a halt and sighs deeply. My body, all but consumed by its hole of hunger, swings around lightly, even as Father moves forward with a suitcase to mount the step. And as I walk away towards the paling I meet the triumphant eyes of the tall boy standing by the whitewashed gate. Above the noise of a car screeching to a halt, the words roll off my tongue disdainfully:

> Why you look and kyk gelyk,
> Am I miskien of gold gemake?
>
> (Why do you look and look simultaneously?
> Am I perhaps made of gold?)

The Toilet

Gcina Mhlope

Sometimes I wanted to give up and be a good girl who listened to her elders. Maybe I should have done something like teaching or nursing as my mother wished. People thought these professions were respectable, but I knew I wanted to do something different, though I was not sure what. I thought a lot about acting. . . . My mother said that it had been a waste of good money educating me because I did not know what to do with the knowledge I had acquired. I'd come to Johannesburg for the December holidays after writing my matric exams, and then stayed on, hoping to find something to do.

My elder sister worked in Orange Grove as a domestic worker, and I stayed with her in her back room. I didn't know anybody in Jo'burg except my sister's friends whom we went to church with. The Methodist church up Fourteenth Avenue was about the only outing we had together. I was very bored and lonely.

On weekdays I was locked in my sister's room so that the Madam wouldn't see me. She was at home most of the time: painting her nails, having tea with her friends, or lying in the sun by the swimming pool. The swimming pool was very close to the room, which is why I had to keep very quiet. My sister felt bad about locking me in there, but she had no alternative. I couldn't even play the radio, so she brought me books, old magazines, and newspapers from the white people. I just read every single thing I came across: *Fair Lady*, *Woman's Weekly*, anything. But then my sister thought I was reading too much.

"What kind of wife will you make if you can't even make baby clothes, or knit yourself a jersey? I suppose you will marry an educated man like yourself, who won't mind going to bed with a book and an empty stomach."

We would play cards at night when she knocked off, and listen to the radio, singing along softly with the songs we liked.

Then I got this temporary job in a clothing factory in town. I looked forward to meeting new people, and liked the idea of being out of that room for a change. The factory made clothes for ladies' boutiques.

The whole place was full of machines of all kinds. Some people were sewing, others were ironing with big heavy irons that pressed with a lot of steam. I had to cut all the loose threads that hang after a dress or a jacket is finished. As soon as a number of dresses in a certain style were finished, they would be sent to me and I had to count them, write the number down, and then start with the cutting of the threads. I was fascinated to discover that one person made only sleeves, another the collars, and so on until the last lady put all the pieces together, sewed on buttons, or whatever was necessary to finish.

Most people at the factory spoke Sotho, but they were nice to me—they tried to speak to me in Zulu or Xhosa, and they gave me all kinds of advice on things I didn't know. There was this girl, Gwendolene—she thought I was very stupid—she called me a "bari" because I always sat inside the changing room with something to read when it was time to eat my lunch, instead of going outside to meet guys. She told me it was cheaper to get myself a "lunch boy"—somebody to buy me lunch. She told me it was wise not to sleep with him, because then I could dump him anytime

I wanted to. I was very nervous about such things. I thought it was better to be a "bari" than to be stabbed by a city boy for his money.

The factory knocked off at four thirty, and then I went to a park near where my sister worked. I waited there till half past six, when I could sneak into the house again without the white people seeing me. I had to leave the house before half past five in the mornings as well. That meant I had to find something to do with the time I had before I could catch the seven-thirty bus to work—about two hours. I would go to a public toilet in the park. For some reason it was never locked, so I would go in and sit on the toilet seat to read some magazine or other until the right time to catch the bus.

The first time I went into this toilet, I was on my way to the bus stop. Usually I went straight to the bus stop outside the OK Bazaars where it was well lit, and I could see. I would wait there, reading, or just looking at the growing number of cars and buses on their way to town. On this day it was raining quite hard, so I thought I would shelter in the toilet until the rain had passed. I knocked first to see if there was anyone inside. As there was no reply, I pushed the door open and went in. It smelled a little—a dryish kind of smell, as if the toilet was not used all that often, but it was quite clean compared to many "Non-European" toilets I knew. The floor was painted red and the walls were cream white. It did not look like it had been painted for a few years. I stood looking around, with the rain coming very hard on the zinc roof. The noise was comforting— to know I had escaped the wet—only a few of the heavy drops had got me. The plastic bag in which I carried my book and purse and neatly folded pink handkerchief was a little damp, but that was because I had used it to cover my head when I ran to the toilet. I pulled my dress down a little so that it would not get creased when I sat down. The closed lid of the toilet was going to be my seat for many mornings after that.

I was really lucky to have found that toilet, because the winter was very cold. Not that it was any warmer in there, but once I'd closed the door it used to be a little less windy. Also the toilet was very small—the walls were wonderfully close to me—it felt like it was made to fit me alone. I enjoyed that kind of privacy. I did a lot of thinking while I sat on that toilet seat. I did a lot of day-dreaming too—many times imagining myself in some big hall doing a really popular play with other young actors. At school, we took set books like *Buzani KuBawo* or *A Man for All Seasons* and made school plays which we toured to the other schools on weekends. I loved it very much. When I was even younger I had done little sketches taken from the Bible and on big days like Good Friday, we acted and sang happily.

I would sit there dreaming. . . .

I was getting bored with the books I was reading—the love stories all sounded the same, and besides that I just lost interest. I started asking myself why I had not written anything since I left school. At least at school I had written some poems, or stories for the school magazine, school competitions and other magazines like *Bona* and *Inkqubela*. Our English teacher was always so encouraging; I remembered the day I showed him my first poem—I was so excited I couldn't concentrate in class for the whole day. I didn't know anything about publishing then, and I didn't ask myself if my stories were good enough. I just enjoyed writing things down when I had the time. So one Friday, after I'd started being that toilet's best customer, I bought myself a notebook in which I was hoping to write something. I didn't use it for quite a while, until one evening.

My sister had taken her usual Thursday afternoon off, and she had delayed somewhere. I came back from work, then waited in the park for the right time to go back into the yard. The white people always had their supper at six thirty and that was the time I used to steal my way in without disturbing them or being seen. My comings and goings had to be secret because they still didn't know I stayed there.

Then I realised that she hadn't come back, and I was scared to go out again, in case something went wrong this time. I decided to sit down in front of my sister's room, where I thought I wouldn't be noticed. I was reading a copy of *Drum Magazine* and hoping that she would come back soon—before the dogs sniffed me out. For the first time I realised how stupid it was of me not to have cut myself a spare key long ago. I kept on hearing noises that sounded like the gate opening. A few times I was sure I had heard her footsteps on the concrete steps leading to the servants' quarters, but it turned out to be something or someone else.

I was trying hard to concentrate on my reading again, when I heard the two dogs playing, chasing each other nearer and nearer to where I was sitting. And then, there they were in front of me, looking as surprised as I was. For a brief moment we stared at each other, then they started to bark at me. I was sure they would tear me to pieces if I moved just one finger, so I sat very still, trying not to look at them, while my heart pounded and my mouth went dry as paper.

They barked even louder when the dogs from next door joined in, glared at me through the openings in the hedge. Then the Madam's high-pitched voice rang out above the dogs' barking.

"Ireeeeeeeene!" That's my sister's English name, which we never use. I couldn't move or answer the call—the dogs were standing right in front of me, their teeth so threateningly long. When there was no reply, she came to see what was going on.

"Oh, it's you? Hello." She was smiling at me, chewing that gum which never left her mouth, instead of calling the dogs away from me. They had stopped barking, but they hadn't moved—they were still growling at me, waiting for her to tell them what to do.

"Please Madam, the dogs will bite me," I pleaded, not moving my eyes from them.

"No, they won't bite you." Then she spoke to them nicely, "Get away now—go on," and they went off. She was like a doll, her hair almost orange in colour, all curls round her madeup face. Her eyelashes fluttered like a doll's. Her thin lips were bright red like her long nails, and she wore very high-heeled shoes. She was still smiling; I wondered if it didn't hurt after a while. When her friends came for a swim, I could always hear her forever laughing at something or other.

She scared me—I couldn't understand how she could smile like that but not want me to stay in her house.

"When did you come in? We didn't see you."

"I've been here for some time now—my sister isn't here. I'm waiting to talk to her."

"Oh—she's not here?" She was laughing, for no reason that I could see. "I can give her a message—you go on home—I'll tell her that you want to see her."

Once I was outside the gate, I didn't know what to do or where to go. I walked slowly, kicking my heels. The streetlights were so very bright! Like big eyes staring at me. I wondered what the people who saw me thought I was doing, walking around at that time of the night. But then I didn't really care, because there wasn't much I could do about the situation right then. I was just thinking how things had to go wrong on that day particularly, because my sister and I were not on such good terms. Early that morning, when the alarm had gone for me to wake up, I did not jump to turn it off, so my sister got really angry with me. She had gone on about me always leaving it to ring for too long, as if it was set for her, and not for me. And when I went out to wash, I had left the door open a second too long, and that was enough to earn me another scolding.

Every morning I had to wake up straight away, roll my bedding and put it all under the bed where my sister was sleeping. I was not supposed to put on the light although it was still dark. I'd light a candle, and tiptoe my way out with a soap dish and a toothbrush. My clothes were on a hanger on a nail at the back of the door. I'd take the hanger and close the door as quietly as I could. Everything had to be ready set the night before. A washing basin full of cold water was also ready outside the door, put there because the sound of running water and the loud screech the taps made in the morning could wake the white people and they would wonder what my sister was doing up so early. I'd do my everything and be off the premises by five thirty with my shoes in my bag—I only put them on once I was safely out of the gate. And that gate made such a noise too. Many times I wished I could jump over it and save myself all that sickening careful-careful business!

Thinking about all these things took my

mind away from the biting cold of the night and my wet nose, until I saw my sister walking towards me.

"Mholo, what are you doing outside in the street?" she greeted me. I quickly briefed her on what had happened.

"Oh Yehovah! You can be so dumb sometimes! What were you doing inside in the first place? You know you should have waited for me so we could walk in together. Then I could say you were visiting or something. Now, you tell me, what am I supposed to say to them if they see you come in again? Hayi!"

She walked angrily towards the gate, with me hesitantly following her. When she opened the gate, she turned to me with an impatient whisper.

"And now why don't you come in, stupid?"

I mumbled my apologies, and followed her in. By some miracle no one seemed to have noticed us, and we quickly munched a snack of cold chicken and boiled potatoes and drank our tea, hardly on speaking terms. I just wanted to howl like a dog. I wished somebody would come and be my friend, and tell me that I was not useless, and that my sister did not hate me, and tell me that one day I would have a nice place to live . . . anything. It would have been really great to have someone my own age to talk to.

But also I knew that my sister was worried for me, she was scared of her employers. If they were to find out that I lived with her, they would fire her, and then we would both be walking up and down the streets. My eleven rand wages wasn't going to help us at all. I don't know how long I lay like that, unable to fall asleep, just wishing and wishing with tears running into my ears.

The next morning I woke up long before the alarm went off, but I just lay there feeling tired and depressed. If there was a way out, I would not have gone to work, but there was this other strong feeling or longing inside me. It was some kind of pain that pushed me to do everything at double speed and run to my toilet. I call it my toilet because that is exactly how I felt about it. It was very rare that I ever saw anybody else go in there in the mornings. It was like they all knew I was using it, and they had to lay off or something. When I went there, I didn't really expect to find it occupied.

I felt my spirits really lifting as I put on my shoes outside the gate. I made sure that my notebook was in my bag. In my haste I even forgot my lunchbox, but it didn't matter. I was walking faster and my feet were feeling lighter all the time.

Then I noticed that the door had been painted, and that a new windowpane had replaced the old broken one. I smiled to myself as I reached the door. Before long I was sitting on that toilet seat, writing a poem.

Many more mornings saw me sitting there writing. Sometimes it did not need to be a poem; I wrote anything that came into my head—in the same way I would have done if I'd had a friend to talk to. I remember some days when I felt like I was hiding something from my sister. She did not know about my toilet in the park, and she was not in the least interested in my notebook.

Then one morning I wanted to write a story about what had happened at work the day before; the supervisor screaming at me for not calling her when I'd seen the people who stole two dresses at lunchtime. I had found it really funny. I had to write about it and I just hoped there were enough pages left in my notebook. It all came back to me, and I was smiling when I reached for the door, but it wouldn't open—it was locked!

I think for the first time I accepted that the toilet was not mine after all. . . . Slowly I walked over to a bench nearby, watched the early spring sun come up, and wrote my story anyway.

The Road to Alexandra

Mark Mathabane

That evening the neighbourhood was gripped by rumors that the Peri-Urban police were going to launch another raid soon, to "clean up" the neighbourhood, so to speak, because the one that morning had been—by police standards—unsuccessful. The back-to-back raids, the rumors went, marked the beginning of the annual "Operation Clean-up Month," a month during which hundreds of black policemen, led by white officers, combed the entire Alexandra ghetto—street by street and yard by yard—searching for people whose passbooks were not in order, gangsters, prostitutes, black families living illegally in the township, shebeen owners and those persons deemed "undesirables" under the Influx Control Law. I did not understand what many of these names meant,

though I was told that we and most of our neighbours were counted under them.

That night we went to sleep with the rumors
of an imminent police raid hanging over the
neighbourhood like a dark cloud.

"We will have to leave before daybreak," I
heard my mother say to my father as we prepared
to go to sleep. "That way when the raid comes
we won't be here." Upon hearing that, Florah
and I tensed and grew frightened. My mother
calmed us.

"Don't believe the rumors, woman," my father
said with an air of authority. "There won't be any
raid. Weren't the police here just today? People
are just scared. They are always scared. They always will be scared."

"But everybody says they're coming," my
mother insisted. "It's the start of Operation Clean-
up Month, remember?"

"Woman," my father said sternly, "I tell you
there won't be any raid. It's just another false
rumor."

But a raid was coming. A little after midnight,
while everybody was sound asleep and snoring and
dreaming, the police invaded the neighbourhood.

"OPEN UP!" Fists banged at the kitchen door.
"IT'S PERI-URBAN!"

For a minute I thought I was dreaming because from outside there suddenly erupted the same volcano of noise of a day ago. Dogs barked. People shrieked and shouted and ran. Sirens screamed. Children screamed. Doors and windows smashed. Feet clumped. I tossed and turned as if in a nightmare, but the persistent pounding and kicking at the door, and the muffled voices coming from the bedroom, convinced me otherwise.

"OPEN UP OR WE'LL BREAK IT DOWN!" demanded the police more loudly.

I slowly crept out from under the blanket; the sheets of newspaper rustled; I felt a tightening in the pit of my stomach, as if a block of ice were embedded there and were now freezing my guts. My sister stirred and whimpered; I reached under the blanket and told her to hush.

"OPEN UP!"

I lost control of my bladder and quickly soaked the cardboard, the newspapers and the blanket. My sleepy eyes strained to make out objects in the dark, but the darkness was impregnable, ominous; the more I stared into it, the blacker and blacker it became. I felt dizzy. I wanted to scream but my voice was paralyzed. Suddenly flashlights flared through the uncurtained window. Glass shattered somewhere nearby. I yearned to become invisible, to have the ground beneath me open and swallow me until it was all over.

"OPEN UP!" a voice bellowed by the window. "WE KNOW YOU'RE IN THERE!"

I succeeded in reaching the bedroom door, fear all over me. I pasted my ear to the door and heard my mother and father whispering to each other in frantic tones. So they were both still in there. How were they going to escape?

"Mama," I whispered frantically, tapping lightly on the door, "the police are here."

"Johannes, is that you?" my mother whispered back.

"They're here, Mama. What should I do?"

"Don't let them in yet."

"But they're breaking the door down, Mama."

"Don't open yet."

"They're breaking it down, Mama."

Silence.

Should I open the door? The police were smashing it, and if I didn't open it their anger would know no bounds once they got in; I remembered well how they beat me up the last time. But my mother and father were attempting to hide, and if I opened too soon they would be taken away; I remembered well how they were taken away the last time. What should I do?

The pounding and kicking at the door awakened my sister, and she started screaming from under the table. After what seemed like an eternity I unlatched the door. As it swung wide open, with tremendous force, two tall black policemen in stiff brown uniforms rushed in and immediately blinded me with the glare from their flashlights. Before I knew what was happening, one of them had kicked me savagely on the side, sending me crashing into a crate in the far corner. I hit the crate with such force that I nearly passed out. With stars in my eyes I grabbed the edges of the crate and tried to rise, but I couldn't; my knees had turned to Jell-O, my eyes were cloudy and my head pounded as if it were being split with an axe. As I tried to gather my senses, another kick sent me back to the floor, flat on my face. As I went down, my jaw struck the blunt side of the blade of an axe jutting from the side of the crate. My head burned with pain. Blood began oozing from my nostrils and lips. Several of my teeth were loose. I started screaming, forgetting all about my father's rule, begging for forgiveness from my assailant for whatever wrong I had done. My bloodied hands reached out and clung to his legs, but he shoved me away. I again lost control of my bladder. My muscles tightened and beads of sweat mingled with blood covered my body. My foggy eyes tried to see where my assailant was and what he was going to do to me next, but I could only make out indistinct shapes and shadows floating like ghosts about the room. Suddenly a crushing, viselike grip clutched my left armpit and jerked me up. I screamed: "Mama!"

"SHUT UP!" the policeman hissed, a hazy shadow of terror towering in front of me. He shook me violently, the glare of his flashlight trained into my eyes, searing them. He jammed me against the brick wall by the ribs, warning me to shut up or else. . . .

"WHAT TOOK YOU SO LONG TO OPEN THE BLOODY DOOR?" he hissed.

"He's had enough, Solly," a deep, surly voice said from somewhere in the room. "He's had enough, let him go."

"DON'T DO IT AGAIN, UNDERSTAND?" my assailant snarled, bringing the flashlight so close to my eyes they seemed to cook. I blinked repeatedly.

"I w-won't d-do i-it a-again." I said with bated breath.

"Where are your parents?" my assailant hissed.

"I d-don't k-know." I felt I had to protect my parents, no matter what.

"You're lying to me, boy!"

"We'll find them, Solly. Let him go. We'll find them."

My assailant let go of me, and I slumped to the floor, spent with fear. I felt the side of my head; it was bruised and swollen, and something pounded like tribal drums inside my ears. My head no longer felt like my head but like a dead weight on my torso. I coughed and spit, and the spittle was all red with blood. My body was wet and slippery with sweat, urine and blood, as if I had been soaked in grease. Feeling dizzy, I leaned against the crate, disbelieving all that was happening, thinking it all a dream—a bad dream— a nightmare, expecting to awaken any time and find that I was unscathed, that nothing had happened.

The lightheadedness dissolved, and I was able to lift my head up again. I saw the two policemen searching the kitchen, kicking chairs, crates, boxes, tins, pots, dishes, rags, cardboard; searching under the table, behind the cupboard, behind the door, in the corners, everywhere; cursing how shabby the place looked, and how everything was hindering their search. Finding no one in the kitchen they went for the bedroom door, where my sister cowered in screams. My heart fluttered, my skin prickled and the tightness in my throat returned. I felt a thick lump of fear force its way down my tight throat, into my tight stomach, where it settled.

One of the policemen grabbed my sister and shoved her away from the door. My sister screamed hysterically and flailed her arms as her owlish eyes searched wildly about the kitchen. She saw me and rushed toward me, urine streaming down her legs. The policeman who had shoved her away now barred her way with his long arms outspread like the wings of some prehistoric bird. He gritted his gleaming teeth at her.

"Where do you think you're going, you little bastard!"

My sister whirled and dove under the table and curled into a tight knot of screaming, helpless, naked fear; there was nothing I could do to protect her or myself. The policeman went over to the table and shook a truncheon in her face, warning her to shut up or else. But my sister was beside herself with fear and did not let up screaming. The policeman left her and strode across the room to the broken window to glance outside. The second policeman meanwhile was struggling to open the bedroom door; apparently my parents had bolted it from within.

"Open up!" he rapped on the door. "Open up or we'll break it down! We know you're in there!" He then paused, expecting his order to be carried out by whoever he thought was inside. It was not. He again seized the doorknob and twisted it violently, but still it would not open. He started pounding the door with his fist and kicking it with his steel-rimmed boots.

"Hey, you bastard." The policeman peering through the window turned to me and demanded to know who was in the bedroom.

"My brother," I said softly.

"Speak up! And who else?"

"I don't know."

"You're lying to me again, boy," he hissed, and started toward me with a raised truncheon. "Your parents are in there, aren't they? No use protecting them, boy, for we'll find them. And when we do"—he smiled fiendishly—"you'll get it."

I remained silent, resigning myself to the worst.

"Now will you stop lying to me, boy." He shook the truncheon in my face.

I tried to say something, to trump up an excuse; my mouth opened wide but no words came out. The policeman lifted his truncheon, and I closed my eyes, expecting a blow; it didn't come. The policeman instead told his comrade to "smash the bloody thing." The other policeman was about to do that anyway, for he had taken several steps away from the door. He flung himself at the door, bursting it at the butt hinges. Streams of perspiration poured down my face. I could scarcely breathe. The policemen had been so thorough in rummaging the kitchen that I had no doubt they would find my parents. There was no way they could possibly have escaped. The window was latticed with iron bars, and there was only the one door.

"There's someone under the bed!" the policeman in the bedroom shouted triumphantly.

"Haul him out!" the policeman by the kitchen window shouted back as he left his station for the bedroom.

"Come out of there, old man! Out, out!"

As he passed me, the policeman who had been standing by the window gave me a wicked look and grinned.

"Hurry up, old man! Come out of there!" the policeman in the bedroom said impatiently. "Hurry, hurry, we haven't got all day!"

"I'm coming, *nkosi*," my father whimpered. They had found him. My mother was sure to be next. What would happen to us children if they took both my mother and father away?

"Who's in there with him?"

"Where's your wife, old man?"

I inched slowly toward the bedroom door, taking care not to attract the attention of the policemen.

"I said, where's your bloody wife, old man?" The question was repeated.

"She's at work, *nkosi*," my father said plaintively. He was standing, naked and head bowed, in the middle of the bedroom. To his right was an old, worn-out wardrobe; to his left a trundle bed with a straw twin-size mattress, upon which George lay, bawling; in front of the bed was an old, flecked brown table, against which my father's interrogator leaned, as he flashed his light all over my father, keeping him blinking all the time.

"At this time of the night?" The question came slowly, ringing with incredulity.

"Yes, *nkosi*."

"What job does she do at two o'clock in the morning?"

"She's a kitchen girl, *nkosi*. She sleeps in. She's a maid in Edenvale."

The interrogator muttered something to himself then said, "Come, let's see your pass."

My father reached for his tattered overalls at the foot of the bed and from the back pocket he removed a small, square, bulky black book and handed it over to the policeman, who hurriedly flipped through it. Stonily, running his eyes up and down my father, he said, "The bloody thing is not in order, you know?"

"Yes, *nkosi*, I know that very much. I didn't pay my poll tax. I was meaning to do so."

"It's not only your poll tax, damn it, old man. Many other things are wrong with it. You know that?"

"Yes, *nkosi*," my father whimpered. "I know that very much. I was meaning to fix them too."

"And I see here that you haven't paid your tribal tax too. Were you meaning to fix that too?" the policeman said sarcastically.

"Yes, *nkosi*." My father's brow started to sweat.

"And the stamp on page fifteen says you're supposed to have a wife here in the city," the policeman said triumphantly, looking at us children, all the time brandishing the bulky black book in my father's face, "What have you to say to that, heh? How are you going to fix that, heh?"

My father became speechless. He parted his parched lips and tried to say something, but no sound came. He lowered his bony head and buried it in the palms of his gnarled hands; and at that moment he seemed to age a thousand years, a pitiful sight. The policeman playfully prodded my father's penis with a truncheon. I gasped with horror.

"Old man," the policeman said floutingly, throwing his head backward, "you're an old man, aren't you?" My father, only in his mid-thirties, nodded. "You're as ancient as my father, yet your irresponsibility makes me ashamed of saying that. Why isn't your pass in order? Mine is. Anyway, look here, as an old man you ought to be back in the Bantustan. My father is back there and living in peace. What are you still doing in the city but asking for trouble?"

The policeman confirmed my suspicions of his being fresh from a tribal reserve. The authorities preferred his kind as policemen because of their ferociousness and blind obedience to white authority. They harboured a twisted fear and hatred of urban blacks; they knew nothing of black solidarity, relishing only the sense of raw power being a policeman gave them over their own kind.

"I'm working, *nkosi*," my father said. "There are no jobs in the Bantustan."

"No jobs in the Bantustan?" the policeman laughed. "What about raising cattle? Or have you forgotten how to do that since coming to the city?"

My father did not answer; he continued gazing at the floor.

"A lot of things are wrong with your pass, and you can be endorsed out at any time, you know that?"

"Yes, *nkosi*, I know that very much."

"Then what do you think we should do with you?"

My father forced a fake smile. It was not a spontaneous smile—my father never smiled. It was a begging smile, a passive acceptance of the policeman's authority. After smiling my father again dropped his eyes to the floor. He seemed uncharacteristically powerless and contrite, a far cry from the tough, resolute and absolute ruler of the house I knew him to be, the father whose words were law. I felt sorry for him. The policeman, still brandishing the bulky black book, leaned into my father's ear and whispered something.

The other policeman meantime was still at the doorjamb, revelling at the sight of my father being humiliated. The emotional and physical nakedness of my father somehow made me see him in a different light—he seemed a stranger, a total alien. Watching him made tears surge to my eyes, but I fought desperately to keep them from flowing. I cannot cry, I told myself, I would not cry, I should not cry in front of these black beasts. For the first time in my life I felt hate and anger rage with furious intensity inside me. What I felt was no ordinary hate or anger; it was something much deeper, much darker, frightening, something even I couldn't understand. As I stood there watching, I could feel that hate and anger being branded into my five-year-old mind, branded to remain until I die.

"Hurry up, old man!" the interrogator said, as my father fidgeted with his overalls. "We haven't got all day. Do you have it or don't you?" he said, trying to wring a bribe out of my father.

"*Nkosi*, I beg you," my father whimpered, drooping his bony shoulders and letting the overalls dangle limply at his side. "I have no money," he sighed.

"Nothing," the policeman cried, astonished; the black policemen were used to getting bribes.

"Nothing, *nkosi*," my father said, slowly running his right hand through his kinky hair. "Not a cent. I have no job. I just applied for a permit to look for a job yesterday."

"Well." The policeman frowned, closing the bulky book in my father's face, "I gave you your chance. You refused it. Now hurry up and put on your clothes and come with us. It's 'Number Four' for you, old man."

"But the little ones—"

"That's none of my bloody business," the policeman cut in sharply. "Tell that to the magistrate. Now hurry up and get dressed!"

My father jumped into his overalls. He was handcuffed.

"Go quiet your brother," he said as he saw me staring at him. I did not go. I watched impassively as they led him through the front door, his head bowed, his hands manacled, his self-esteem drained, his manhood sapped. I wondered where they were taking him, what grievous wrong had he committed deserving of being shackled, what type of fiends the two policemen were. They weren't humans to me, neither were they black. Though I feared them as one would fear monsters, I didn't let fear panic me, for I hated them more than I feared them.

Curious to find out where they were taking my father, and what was going on outside, I followed them, forgetting all about my mother. I ordered my sister, who was crying, "Papa, Papa!" by the door, back into the house. I stepped outside in time to see the two policemen, flanking my father, go up a rocky slope leading out of the yard. I saw more black policemen leading black men and women out of shacks. Some of the prisoners were half naked, others dressed as they went. Several children, two and three years old, stood in tears outside smashed doors, imploring their mothers and fathers to come back. In the middle of the yard an old man was being shoved by a black policeman for being slow; a woman was being kicked by another black policeman for being stubborn; another woman was being ordered to leave a bawling infant behind. Several red-necked white men in safari suits and fatigues, guns drawn, paced briskly about the entrance gate, shouting orders and supervising the roundup. I avoided them by going around the shacks. On my way to the gate I passed shacks whose windows had been shattered, whose doors had been busted. The interiors of some of the shacks were a mess, as if a tornado had hit. I arrived at the gate and found a group of boys in a half circle on a stoep overlooking the street.

Dawn was starting to break but stars still twinkled faintly in the distant, pale eastern sky. PUTCO buses droned in the distance, carrying loads of black humanity to the white world to work. I joined the group of boys. My eyes wandered up, then down the street. I gasped at what I saw down the street. A huge throng of handcuffed black men and women, numbering in the hundreds, filled the narrow street from side to side. The multitude, murmuring like herds of restless cattle, was being marched by scores of black policemen and a dozen or so white ones, some of whom had fierce police dogs on leashes, toward a row of about ten police vans and trucks parked farther down the street. More handcuffed men and women were still filing out of the yards on either side, swelling the ranks of those already choking the streets. It seemed as if the entire population of Alexandra had been arrested.

As I stood there, openmouthed with fearful anticipation, watching the handcuffed men and women being shoved, jostled, kicked and thrown like bundles into the trucks and vans, along with the dogs, I saw, out of the corner of my eye, a short, potbellied black policeman leading a naked black man with bony, stiltlike legs, out of an outhouse in a yard across the street. The naked man pleaded that he be allowed to go and dress, but the fat policeman simply roared with laughter and prodded the naked man in the back with a truncheon, telling him that it was not his fault that he had caught him naked.

"Next time hide with your clothes on, brother," the policeman jeered.

The boys around me giggled at the sight of the naked man being marched down the street, toward the throng of handcuffed men and women, his gnarled hands cupped between his bony legs. I remained silent. A tall black man standing by the gate to one of the yards overlooking the street—one of the few adults left behind, presumably because his papers were in order—saw the naked man and instantly dashed into his house and came out waving a pair of tattered overalls. He hurled them across the *donga*, and they landed in the middle of the street, a few paces from the approaching policeman and his naked captive. Grudgingly, amid shouts of "Hurry up, we haven't got all day," intended to please the group of women prisoners gaping at the scene from a short distance, the policeman allowed the naked man to pick up the overalls. He dressed in the middle of the street.

Meanwhile the truck and vans, now jam-packed with handcuffed men and women and dogs and black policemen, hummed engines and prepared to leave. More handcuffed men and women and policemen and dogs still remained in the streets. Within minutes more vans and trucks came, and the loading was finally completed. The convoy of vans and trucks sped away in a huge cloud of dust, with several of the black policemen dangling from the side and rear doors like rags on a line.

As the group dispersed, some of the boys started talking in soft, subdued tones.

"They've taken my father away."

"They've taken my mother and father."

"They've taken my brother."

"They've taken my sister."

"They've taken my whole family."

"They've taken my aunt and uncle."

"They've taken my mother and left my father after he had given them some money."

Mother! Where was my mother? All along I had been oblivious of her. Remembering that the police did not find her when they searched the house, I ran back home as fast as I could to try and find her. I found my brother and sister still crying, but I ignored them.

"Mama! Where are you?" I shouted, standing in the middle of the bedroom. "They're gone."

No reply.

I repeated the shout. The wardrobe creaked and a voice inside softly asked, "Are they gone?"

Instantly I leaped back; my eyes popped out in fearful astonishment.

"Mama, is that you?" I warily approached the wardrobe.

"Yes, let me out!"

"Mama, are you in there?" I said, to make sure that I had indeed heard her voice. I could not believe she had hidden herself in so small a wardrobe. My sister and I often had trouble fitting in there whenever we played hide-and-seek.

"Yes, let me out!"

"It's locked, Mama. Where's the key?"

My mother told me that my father had it. I told her he was gone. She remained silent for a moment or two and then told me to look for it on the table. I looked; no key. I told her so. She told me to look where my father had been hiding. Flickering candle in hand, I crawled under the bed to the far corner where my father had been hiding but I found no key on the earthen floor. Where was the key? Had my father unwittingly taken it with him? How would I get my mother out? "There's no key where he was, Mama!" I shouted from under the bed.

"Look again!"—pause—"and thoroughly this time!"

Before resuming the search I spat twice on my right palm and parted the spittle with my left forefinger, watching to see where the most spit went. It went to the right. I then uttered the supplication my mother had taught me. "Ancestors! Ancestors! Guide me to whatever I'm looking for, wherever it may lie!" I concentrated my search on the right side of the bed. Still no key. I became frantic.

"There's no key, Mama."

She told me to look everywhere. I began ransacking the house and while overturning the torn straw mattress I found a pair of old, rusted keys in one of the holes. I tried them on the wardrobe lock; they wouldn't even fit. Finally, in exasperation, I went to the kitchen, grabbed a heavy wood axe and went back to the bedroom, determined to chop the wardrobe down and get my mother out.

"Mama, should I chop the door down and let you out?" I said fervently. Florah, standing nearby, shrieked with horror as I lifted the axe.

"NO!" my mother shrieked from inside the wardrobe.

"What should I do then?"

"LOOK AGAIN!"

"Look where? I've looked everywhere."

"LOOK AGAIN UNDER THE BED!"

"I've looked there twice already. There's nothing there."

"LOOK AGAIN CAREFULLY!"

"Please look again, Johannes," my sister begged. "I'll help you look."

"Shut up, you!"

Reluctantly, I leaned the axe against the wardrobe door and crawled back under the bed. "For ancestors' sake," I cried, "where's the key!" I was now convinced that my father had unwittingly taken it with him. If he had, what then? My mother would just have to let me chop down the door. Didn't my father always say I chopped wood like a man?

I don't know what made me look between the bricks propping up one leg of the bed, but in one of the crevices I found a long, glistening key, along with several farthings, which I pocketed. The key slid easily into the lock. I turned it twice to the right, and then the knob; they both turned easily. The door swung open. My mother, clad only in her underwear, wriggled out from the tiny compartment where clothes would have been hanging, had we had any worth hanging. She stretched her numb legs and cracked her neck and back. She then dressed and quieted my brother by letting him suckle. Afterward she went about the task of restoring a semblance of order to the mess the police had created.

My father spent two months doing hard labour on a white man's potato farm for his pass crimes.

A Chip of Glass Ruby

Nadine Gordimer

When the duplicating machine was brought into the house, Bamjee said, "Isn't it enough that you've got the Indians' troubles on your back?" Mrs. Bamjee said, with a smile that showed the gap of a missing tooth but was confident all the same, "What's the difference, Yusuf? We've all got the same troubles."

"Don't tell me that. We don't have to carry passes; let the natives protest against passes on their own, there are millions of them. Let them go ahead with it."

The nine Bamjee and Pahad children were present at this exchange as they were always; in the small house that held them all there was no room for privacy for the discussion of matters they were too young to hear, and so they had never been too young to hear anything. Only their sister and half-sister, Girlie, was missing; she was the eldest, and married. The children looked expectantly, unalarmed and interested, at Bamjee, who had neither left the room nor settled down again to the task of rolling his own cigarettes, which had been interrupted by the arrival of the duplicator. He had looked at the thing that had come hidden in a wash basket and conveyed in a black man's taxi, and the children turned on it too, their black eyes surrounded by thick lashes like those still, open flowers with hairy tentacles that close on whatever touches them.

"A fine thing to have on the table where we eat," was all he said at last. They smelled the machine among them; a smell of cold black grease. He went out, heavily on tiptoe, in his troubled way.

"It's going to go nicely on the sideboard!" Mrs. Bamjee was busy making a place by removing the two pink glass vases filled with plastic carnations and the hand-painted velvet runner with the picture of the Taj Mahal.

After supper she began to run off leaflets on the machine. The family lived in that room—the three other rooms in the house were full of beds—and they were all there. The older children shared a bottle of ink while they did their homework, and the two little ones pushed a couple of empty milk bottles in and out the chair legs. The three-year-old fell asleep and was carted away by one of the girls. They all drifted off to bed eventually; Bamjee himself went before the older children— he was a fruit-and-vegetable hawker and was up at half past four every morning to get to the market by five. "Not long now," said Mrs. Bamjee. The older children looked up and smiled at him. He turned his back on her. She still wore the traditional clothing of a Moslem woman, and her body, which was scraggy and unimportant as a dress on a peg when it was not host to a child, was wrapped in the trailing rags of a cheap sari and her thin black plait was greased. When she was a girl, in the Transvaal town where they lived still, her mother fixed a chip of glass ruby in her nostril; but she had abandoned that adornment as too old-style, even for her, long ago.

She was up until long after midnight, turning out leaflets. She did it as if she might have been pounding chillies.

Bamjee did not have to ask what the leaflets were. He had read the papers. All the past week Africans had been destroying their passes and then presenting themselves for arrest. Their leaders were jailed on charges of incitement, campaign offices were raided—someone must be helping the few minor leaders who were left to keep the campaign going without offices or equipment. What was it the leaflets would say—"Don't go to work tomorrow," "Day of Protest," "Burn Your Pass for Freedom"? He didn't want to see.

He was used to coming home and finding his wife sitting at the table deep in discussion with strangers or people whose names were familiar by repute. Some were prominent Indians, like the lawyer, Dr. Abdul Mohammed Khan, or the big businessman, Mr. Moonsamy Patel, and he was flattered, in a suspicious way, to meet them in his house. As he came home from work next day he met Dr. Khan coming out of the house and Dr. Khan—a highly educated man—said to him, "A wonderful woman." But Bamjee had never caught his wife out in any presumption; she behaved properly, as any Moslem woman should, and once her business with such gentlemen was over would never, for instance, have sat down to eat with them. He found her now back in the kitchen, setting about the preparation of dinner and carrying on a conversation on several different wavelengths with the children. "It's really a shame if you're tired of lentils, Jimmy, because that's what you're getting—Amina, hurry up, get a pot of water going—don't worry, I'll mend that in a minute, just bring the yellow cotton, and there's a needle in the cigarette box on the sideboard."

"Was that Dr. Khan leaving?" said Bamjee.

"Yes, there's going to be a stay-at-home on Monday. Desai's ill, and he's got to get the word around by himself. Bob Jali was up all last night printing leaflets, but he's gone to have a tooth out." She had always treated Bamjee as if it were only a mannerism that made him appear uninterested in politics, the way some woman will persist in interpreting her husband's bad temper as an endearing gruffness hiding boundless goodwill, and she talked to him of these things just as she passed on to him neighbours' or family gossip.

"What for do you want to get mixed up with these killings and stonings and I don't know what? Congress should keep out of it. Isn't it enough with the Group Areas?"

She laughed. "Now, Yusuf, you know you don't believe that. Look how you said the same thing when the Group Areas started in Natal. You said we should begin to worry when we get moved out of our own houses here in the Transvaal. And then your mother lost her house in Noorddorp, and there you are; you saw that nobody's safe.

Oh, Girlie was here this afternoon, she says Ismail's brother's engaged—that's nice, isn't it? His mother will be pleased; she was worried."

"Why was she worried?" asked Jimmy, who was fifteen, and old enough to patronize his mother.

"Well, she wanted to see him settled. There's a party on Sunday week at Ismail's place—you'd better give me your suit to give to the cleaners tomorrow, Yusuf."

One of the girls presented herself at once. "I'll have nothing to wear, Ma."

Mrs. Bamjee scratched her sallow face. "Perhaps Girlie will lend you her pink, eh? Run over to Girlie's place now and say I say will she lend it to you."

The sound of commonplaces often does service as security, and Bamjee, going to sit in the armchair with the shiny armrests that was wedged between the table and the sideboard, lapsed into an unthinking doze that, like all times of dreamlike ordinariness during those weeks, was filled with uneasy jerks and starts back into reality. The next morning, as soon as he got to market, he heard that Dr. Khan had been arrested. But that night Mrs. Bamjee sat up making a new dress for her daughter; the sight disarmed Bamjee, reassured him again, against his will, so that the resentment he had been making ready all day faded into a morose and accusing silence. Heaven knew, of course, who came and went in the house during the day. Twice in that week of riots, raids and arrests, he found black women in the house when he came home; plain ordinary native women in doeks, drinking tea. This was not a thing other Indian women would have in their homes, he thought bitterly; but then his wife was not like other people, in a way he could not put his finger on, except to say what it was not: not scandalous, not punishable, not rebellious. It was, like the attraction that had led him to marry her, Pahad's widow with five children, something he could not see clearly.

When the Special Branch knocked steadily on the door in the small hours of Thursday morning he did not wake up, for his return to consciousness was always set in his mind to half past four, and that was more than an hour away. Mrs. Bamjee got up herself, struggled into Jimmy's raincoat which was hanging over a chair and went to the front door. The clock on the wall—a wedding present when she married Pahad—showed three o'clock when she snapped on the light, and she knew at once who it was on the other side of the door. Although she was not surprised, her hands shook like a very old person's as she undid the locks and the complicated catch on the wire burglarproofing. And then she opened the door and they were there—two coloured policemen in plain clothes. "Zanip Bamjee?"

"Yes."

As they talked, Bamjee woke up in the sudden terror of having overslept. Then he became conscious of men's voices. He heaved himself out of bed in the dark and went to the window, which, like the front door, was covered with a heavy mesh of thick wire against intruders from the dingy lane it looked upon. Bewildered, he appeared in the room, where the policemen were searching through a soapbox of papers beside the duplicating machine. "Yusuf, it's for me," Mrs. Bamjee said.

At once, the snap of a trap, realization came. He stood there in an old shirt before the two policemen, and the woman was going off to prison because of the natives. "There you are!" he shouted, standing away from her. "That's what you've got for it. Didn't I tell you? Didn't I? That's the end of it now. That's the finish. That's what it's come to." She listened with her head at the slightest tilt to one side, as if to ward off a blow, or in compassion.

Jimmy, Pahad's son, appeared at the door with a suitcase; two or three of the girls were behind him. "Here, Ma, you take my green jersey." "I've found your clean blouse." Bamjee had to keep moving out of their way as they helped their mother to make ready. It was like the preparation for one of the family festivals his wife made such a fuss over; wherever he put himself, they bumped into him. Even the two policemen mumbled, "Excuse me," and pushed past into the rest of the house to continue their search. They took with them a tome that Nehru had written in prison; it had been bought from a persevering travelling salesman and kept, for years, on the mantelpiece. "Oh, don't take that, please," Mrs. Bamjee said suddenly, clinging to the arm of the man who had picked it up.

The man held it away from her.

"What does it matter, Ma?"

It was true that no one in the house had ever read it; but she said, "It's for my children."

"Ma, leave it." Jimmy, who was squat and plump, looked like a merchant advising a client against a roll of silk she had set her heart on. She went into the bedroom and got dressed. When she came out in her old yellow sari with a brown coat over it, the faces of the children were behind her like faces on the platform at a railway station. They kissed her goodbye. The policemen did not hurry her, but she seemed to be in a hurry just the same.

"What am I going to do?" Bamjee accused them all.

The policemen looked away patiently.

"It'll be all right. Girlie will help. The big children can manage. And Yusuf—" The children crowded in around her; two of the younger ones had awakened and appeared, asking shrill questions.

"Come on," said the policemen.

"I want to speak to my husband." She broke away and came back to him, and the movement of her sari hid them from the rest of the room for a moment. His face hardened in suspicious anticipation against the request to give some message to the next fool who would take up her pamphleteering until he, too, was arrested. "On Sunday," she said. "Take them on Sunday." He did not know what she was talking about. "The engagement party," she whispered, low and urgent. "They shouldn't miss it. Ismail will be offended."

They listened to the car drive away. Jimmy bolted and barred the front door, and then at once opened it again; he put on the raincoat that

his mother had taken off. "Going to tell Girlie,"
he said. The children went back to bed. Their
father did not say a word to any of them; their
talk, the crying of the younger ones and the ar-
gumentative voices of the older, went on in the
bedrooms. He found himself alone; he felt the
night all around him. And then he happened to
meet the clock face and saw with a terrible sense
of unfamiliarity that this was not the secret night
but an hour he should have recognized: the time
he always got up. He pulled on his trousers and
his dirty white hawker's coat and wound his grey
muffler up to the stubble on his chin and went to
work.

The duplicating machine was gone from the sideboard. The policemen had taken it with them,
along with the pamphlets and the conference re-
ports and the stack of old newspapers that had
collected on top of the wardrobe in the bedroom—
not the thick dailies of the white men but the
thin, impermanent-looking papers that spoke up,
sometimes interrupted by suppression or lack of
money, for the rest. It was all gone. When he
had married her and moved in with her and her
five children, into what had been the Pahad and
became the Bamjee house, he had not recognized

the humble, harmless and apparently useless routine tasks—the minutes of meetings being written up on the dining-room table at night, the government blue books that were read while the latest baby was suckled, the employment of the fingers of the older children in the fashioning of crinkle-paper Congress rosettes—as activity intended to move mountains. For years and years he had not noticed it, and now it was gone.

The house was quiet. The children kept to their lairs, crowded on the beds with the doors shut. He sat and looked at the sideboard, where the plastic carnations and the mat with the picture of the Taj Mahal were in place. For the first few weeks he never spoke of her. There was the feeling, in the house, that he had wept and raged at her, that boulders of reproach had thundered down upon her absence, and yet he had said not one word. He had not been to inquire where she was; Jimmy and Girlie had gone to Mohammed Ebrahim, the lawyer, and when he found out that their mother had been taken—when she was arrested, at least—to a prison in the next town, they had stood about outside the big prison door for hours while they waited to be told where she had been moved from there. At last they had discovered that she was fifty miles away, in Pretoria. Jimmy asked Bamjee for five shillings to help Girlie pay the train fare to Pretoria, once she had been interviewed by the police and had been given a permit to visit her mother; he put three two-shilling pieces on the table for Jimmy to pick up, and the boy, looking at him keenly, did not know whether the extra shilling meant anything, or whether it was merely that Bamjee had no change.

It was only when relations and neighbours came to the house that Bamjee would suddenly begin to talk. He had never been so expansive in his life as he was in the company of these visitors, many of them come on a polite call rather in the nature of a visit of condolence. "Ah, yes, yes, you can see how I am —you see what has been done to me. Nine children, and I am on the cart all day. I get home at seven or eight. What are you to do? What can people like us do?"

"Poor Mrs. Bamjee. Such a kind lady."

"Well, you see for yourself. They walk in here in the middle of the night and leave a houseful of children. I'm out on the cart all day, I've got a living to earn." Standing about in his shirt sleeves, he became quite animated; he would call for the girls to bring fruit drinks for the visitors. When they were gone, it was as if he, who was orthodox if not devout and never drank liquor, had been drunk and abruptly sobered up; he looked dazed and could not have gone over in his mind what he had been saying. And as he cooled, the lump of resentment and wrongedness stopped his throat again.

Bamjee found one of the little boys the centre of a self-important group of championing brothers and sisters in the room one evening. "They've been cruel to Ahmed."

"What has he done?" said the father.

"Nothing! Nothing!" The little girl stood twisting her handkerchief excitedly.

An older one, thin as her mother, took over, silencing the others with a gesture of her skinny hand. "They did it at school today. They made an example of him."

"What is an example?" said Bamjee impatiently.

"The teacher made him come up and stand in front of the whole class, and he told them, 'You see this boy? His mother's in jail because she likes the natives so much. She wants the Indians to be the same as natives.'"

"It's terrible," he said. His hands fell to his sides. "Did she ever think of this?"

"That's why Ma's *there*," said Jimmy, putting aside his comic and emptying out his schoolbooks upon the table. "That's all the kids need to know. Ma's there because things like this happen. Petersen's a coloured teacher, and it's his black blood that's brought him trouble all his life, I suppose. He hates anyone who says everybody's the same because that takes away from him his bit of whiteness that's all he's got. What d'you expect? It's nothing to make too much fuss about."

"Of course, you are fifteen and you know everything," Bamjee mumbled at him.

"I don't say that. But I know Ma, anyway." The boy laughed.

There was a hunger strike among the political prisoners, and Bamjee could not bring himself to ask Girlie if her mother was starving herself too. He would not ask; and yet he saw in the young woman's face the gradual weakening of her mother. When the strike had gone on for nearly a week one of the elder children burst into tears at the table and could not eat. Bamjee pushed his own plate away in rage.

Sometimes he spoke out loud to himself while he was driving the vegetable lorry. "What for?" Again and again: "What for?" She was not a modern woman who cut her hair and wore short skirts. He had married a good plain Moslem woman who bore children and stamped her own chillies. He had a sudden vision of her at the duplicating machine, that night just before she was taken away, and he felt himself maddened, baffled and hopeless. He had become the ghost of a victim, hanging about the scene of a crime whose motive he could not understand and had not had time to learn.

The hunger strike at the prison went into the second week. Alone in the rattling cab of his lorry, he said things that he heard as if spoken by some-one else, and his heart burned in fierce agreement with them. "For a crowd of natives who'll smash our shops and kill us in our houses when their time comes." "She will starve herself to death there." "She will die there." "Devils who will burn and kill us." He fell into bed each night like a stone, and dragged himself up in the mornings as a beast of burden is beaten to its feet.

One of these mornings, Girlie appeared very early, while he was wolfing bread and strong tea—alternate sensations of dry solidity and stinging heat—at the kitchen table. Her real name was Fatima, of course, but she had adopted the silly modern name along with the clothes of the young factory girls among whom she worked. She was expecting her first baby in a week or two, and her small face, her cut and curled hair and the sooty arches drawn over her eyebrows did not seem to belong to her thrust-out body under a clean smock. She wore mauve lipstick and was smiling her cocky little white girl's smile, foolish and bold, not like an Indian girl's at all.

"What's the matter?" he said.

She smiled again. "Don't you know? I told Bobby he must get me up in time this morning. I wanted to be sure I wouldn't miss you today."

"I don't know what you're talking about."

She came over and put her arm up around his unwilling neck and kissed the grey bristles at the side of his mouth. "Many happy returns! Don't you know it's your birthday?"

"No," he said. "I didn't know, didn't think—" He broke the pause by swiftly picking up the bread and giving his attention desperately to eating and drinking. His mouth was busy, but his eyes looked at her, intensely black. She said nothing, but stood there with him. She would not speak, and at last he said, swallowing a piece of bread that tore at his throat as it went down, "I don't remember these things."

The girl nodded, the Woolworth baubles in her ears swinging. "That's the first thing she told me when I saw her yesterday—don't forget it's Bajie's birthday tomorrow."

He shrugged over it. "It means a lot to children. But that's how she is. Whether it's one of the old cousins or the neighbour's grandmother, she always knows when the birthday is. What importance is my birthday, while she's sitting there in a prison? I don't understand how she can do the things she does when her mind is always full of woman's nonsense at the same time—that's what I don't understand with her."

"Oh, but don't you see?" the girl said. "It's because she doesn't want anybody to be left out. It's because she always remembers; remembers everything—people without somewhere to live, hungry kids, boys who can't get educated—remembers all the time. That's how Ma is."

"Nobody else is like that." It was half a complaint.

"No, nobody else," said his stepdaughter.

She sat herself down at the table, resting her belly. He put his head in his hands. "I'm getting old"—but he was overcome by something much more curious, by an answer. He knew why he had desired her, the ugly widow with five children; he knew what way it was in which she was not like the others; it was there, like the fact of the belly that lay between him and her daughter.

A Farm at Raraba

Ernst Havemann

My late Dad was a magnificent shot. One time when we were hunting in the Low Veld and had paused for a smoke, there was the yelp of a wild dog, and a troop of impala came bounding over the tall grass. Opposite us, three hundred yards off, was a stony ridge like a wall, six feet high. You would think those buck would avoid it, but no, they went straight at it. One after the other, without pausing or swerving, they leapt over it. They cleared it by three or four feet. I tell you, friend, it was a beautiful sight. You can't beat Nature for beauty, eh.

By the time the first two impala were over the ridge, late Dad was ready, and as the next one leapt, Dad got him. In midair. Same with the next one, and the next, and the next.. And the next. And the next. That was six buck, one after the other.

Do you know, the wild dogs chasing those buck didn't pause for the impala that late Dad had killed. They didn't even react to the shots. They just followed one particular buck that they had marked, and we saw them pull it down a couple of minutes later. You've got to hand it to Nature; she knows what she's doing.

But the most wonderful thing was when we got to the dead impala. Four of them were piled one on top of the other, neatly, like sacks in a store. Late Dad had shot each of them through the heart, at exactly the same point in its leap. The other two had been a bit slow. Late Dad had got each of them in the shoulder. If you can't get a head or a heart shot, the next best is the shoulder, because there's a lot of bone there, and if you hit bone it brings a creature down. It can't run, you see. The worst place is behind the heart, because then your bullet goes through a lot of soft entrails, eh. A gut-shot animal will sometimes run a couple of miles before it drops and you may never find it. When I hear of fellows shooting like that, it makes me want to put a slug into their guts and see how they would like to die that way.

Those impala were a bit of a problem. We only

had a license for two and we only had the two mules we were riding. But God sent the ravens to Elijah, eh, so he sent us this Hottentot, Khamatjie. He worked crops on a share on the same farm as late Dad, but he was luckier with his farming—they live on the smell of an oil rag, those bastards. I don't mean "bastard" in a nasty way. I just mean there was a white father or grandfather, you understand. Well, thank God, this Khamatjie pitches up with his Ford pickup and a mincing machine, because he thought he would shoot a zebra. Nobody wants to eat zebra, but when it's sausage it's lovely; you call it beef or koodoo or eland. Late Dad and Khamatjie and I made impala sausages for two days.

In front of other white people Dad always treated Khamatjie like dirt, but otherwise he was very respectful, because he was always borrowing money from Khamatjie and getting drunk with him. He said Khamatjie didn't mind supplying the brandy so long as he could say he drank with a white man.

The training late Dad gave me in bushcraft and using a rifle came in pretty handy when I was on the border of South-West, doing my army service. The call-up interrupts a man's career, if he's got a career, but a fellow that hasn't had army has missed an experience—the outdoor life, learning about musketry and map reading and section leading, and who's what in these little frontline states, and the tribes and the various movements in Angola and Caprivi and Botswana. The big thing, though, is the companionship. Until you've marched with four hundred other chaps, all in step, all singing "Sarie Marais" or "Lili Marlene" or "You can do with your loo loo what you will"— until you've sat with five or six buddies in an ambush, not daring to take a breath in case a guerrilla gets you—until you've done things like that, you don't know what loving your land and your folk is.

Out there, in the bundu, the action is sort of clean, like they say it was in North Africa when we were fighting Rommel in late Dad's war. Not like shooting little black schoolgirls in the bum from inside an armored car. How brave does a fellow have to be for that? I wonder what these township heroes would do if they were faced with Swapo guerrillas like my lot were.

Because I was keen and liked the bush, eh, I got to be a sergeant, and they gave me six munts they had scratched up in Damaraland, and sent us off across the border into Angola. An intelligence probe, they said. Just these six munts, and me, and an intelligence corporal named Johan. He had had a course of interrogation training and his main job was to train these munts to get information out of prisoners. Scary stuff, man. You've got to hate a person to do it properly, or just hate people, eh.

Our first ten days on patrol yielded nothing. Then on the eleventh day, I had left Johan and the munts to fix our bivvie for the night while I went ahead for a look-see, at a big granite outcrop about two miles ahead. Just before I got to it there were shots from our camp, then some answering shots, then silence. I hid and waited quietly. After five minutes I saw four Swaples, running for all they were worth, along the side of a kopje half a mile away. They disappeared behind a dune, then bunched up on the big granite outcrop before the first Swapie launched himself off it to cross a crevasse. By that time I was ready, and I got him as he jumped. The next one was too close behind to stop, and I dropped him and number three as fast as it takes to press the trigger. The last one in the bunch pulled back, but I was quick and ready. I hit him, too. I heard the bullet ricochet off the rock, so I reckoned he was probably only wounded.

I was sure the first three would be dead, and I

thought, Late Dad, look at that! Three in midair! And they're not impala, Dad. They're Royal Game.

Do you know about Royal Game? Late Dad told me, in the old days, before we became the Republic, anything that you were not allowed to shoot, because it was rare or useful, like tickbirds or ibises or oribi, was called Royal Game. Kids in those days believed it was because these birds or animals were reserved for the Royal Family to shoot. Fancy Prince Charles potting away at a flock of egrets or an iguana, eh! So Dad and his friends called desert natives Royal Game, because they are wild but you're not allowed to shoot them, see?

Like I told you, man, I can't bear to think of a gut-shot animal, lying in pain for hours. I felt the same way about this guerrilla, but I was on edge too. They say a wounded lion or buffalo is the most dangerous game in the wild, because he stalks the hunter. A wounded munt guerrilla must be worse, because he's got more IQ, eh, so I circled very cautiously round the granite rock. When I got opposite the crevasse I could see three bodies, one on top of the other, quite still. At eight hundred yards, three in three shots, it's a satisfaction, man.

And there, thank God, was guerrilla number four, just round the corner. He was standing upright in a narrow cleft in the rock, with one foot apparently stuck, and he was gripping his left bicep. A pressure point, I supposed. Through my field glasses I could see his left sleeve was a thick mat of blood. So all I had got was his arm. I found myself making excuses, thinking I had been slow because I used a peepsight. Late Dad always shot over open sights; he reckoned a sniper's eye aimed his hand, like a cowboy with a pistol, or a kid with a catapult.

The guerrilla's rifle was wedged above his head. For safety's sake I put a bullet into it. That left him unlikely to do much damage. When I edged my way closer I saw his leg was held fast in a crack, so he really was stuck and helpless. He was one of those yellow Hottentot types, with spaces between his peppercorns of hair, about my age but as wrinkled as a prune. These Kalahari natives go like that by the time they're twenty: it's the sun or glands, I don't know. He was wearing a cast-off Cuban tunic.

I climbed up the rock and looked down on him, trying to remember the few words of local lingo I had picked up from my men, but when he heard me he said in Afrikaans, "Good day, my baas."

I was pleased, I can tell you. It meant I could interrogate him myself and, as he was our first prisoner, it would show Johan and my black soldiers that I was one step ahead of them, and it wasn't for nothing I was a sergeant.

The guerrilla bowed his head and pointed with his good hand. "If you are going to shoot, make it two shots, please, so that I will be properly dead."

"I don't shoot tethered goats," I said.

After a moment or two he looked up. "Can the goat have some water?"

"First, talk."

"Yes, I talk, baas. What would baas like to talk about?"

I interrogated him, in the way we had been instructed, using trick questions and repetitions. In case he was lying or hiding anything I prodded his wounded arm once or twice. He bore it as if he had it coming to him, but he didn't appear to keep information back, and when his voice cracked I passed down my water bottle.

His name was Adoons, which is a jokey way of saying Adonis. It is what one calls a pet baboon. The farmer his family had worked for called him that. Eventually his own family stopped using the native name his father gave him and almost forgot it. It seemed to belong to someone else, Adoons said.

He had been a hunters' guide and a shepherd. When his family was pushed off the farm—for sheep stealing, it seemed—he joined the guerrillas who were fighting for Namibian independence. He had only the vaguest idea what the fighting was about. He knew it was against whites, but he had never heard of Namibia. Not surprising, when you think that there is no such place. He called it "South-West," just like we do. He moved from one guerrilla band to another, depending on how he liked the band's leader, and how much food or loot was available. His present band was under an Ndebele refugee from Zimbabwe. They were supposed to report to a General Kareo, but they had never seen him. I carefully recorded it all in my field notebook.

When I had done with questions, I sat back and lighted a cigarette. At the sound of the match he looked up. Smoking alone or drinking alone is not something a decent man wants to do; it's like making love alone, late Dad used to say. I gave Adoons the cigarette and lighted another one for myself.

He exhaled till his chest was flat, and then inhaled the smoke to fill his lungs. He held it for a long time before letting it out and saying, "Thank you, baas. Baas is a good man."

He smoked in deep gulps, keeping his head down. When he finished the cigarette he looked up. "Why didn't baas shoot when I was full of smoke?"

"I told you I don't shoot jackal bait," I said.

"I can see baas is a good man, but if baas's men find me here, they will do bad things to me. Perhaps it will take three days."

"I will tell them you have already talked."

"They will not care. They will torture me to make a game. My people will do it, too, if they catch one of your black soldiers. This is not Sunday school, my baas."

"We don't torture prisoners," I replied angrily. I knew he would not believe me.

"What will baas do with me?"

The fact was I didn't know what the hell I could do with Adoons. Once he has been interrogated, a native prisoner is worthless—worse, he would be a danger. He would have to be fed and guarded, and if he escaped he could give the enemy all sorts of valuable information. We didn't keep prisoners, except white men and Cubans: you could exchange or use them for propaganda.

As if sharing my problem, he said, "Has baas

perhaps room for another shepherd on baas's farm?"

"I haven't got a farm, and if I wanted a shepherd I would not employ a bloody Hottentot rebel."

"It is near sunset. Baas will go soon, before it gets dark. And when baas goes the hyenas will come. A hyena can bite right through a man's leg. A living man's leg."

I looked down at his skinny leg disappearing into the rock cleft, then climbed down and looked at his imprisoned foot. All I had to do was untie the laces and manipulate his ankle to get his foot out, leaving the boot behind. Then I gave the empty boot a kick and it came loose, too. Adoons wriggled till he found a purchase for his toes and raised himself a few inches.

"Give me your hand, Hottentot," I said. "I'll pull you out."

He put up his hand. I took him by the wrist and he clasped my wrist. With unexpected agility he braced his feet against the side of the cleft and scrambled up. I threw him his boot. When he stood up to catch it, his tunic opened to reveal a pistol loose in a leather holster on a broad, stylish belt round his waist.

He smiled shamefacedly. "I took it from the policeman who arrest me for stealing sheep."

"Is it loaded?"

"Oh, yes. Five bullets. I used one to learn to shoot it, but I've never fired it since. One has to be close to a man."

"You could have shot me."

"Yes, my baas. The pistol was stuck fast, like me, but when you were asking all those questions and leaning down to hear what I was saying, the barrel was pointing straight at you."

"Why didn't you shoot?"

"If baas was dead I would still be stuck in that rock with no one to help me before the soldiers or the hyenas came."

His wounded arm had been banged as he made his way up. It now began to bleed through the clot, not actively but *clthip, clthip, clthip.* Since I carried three field dressings, I could spare one. I dusted the antiseptic powder that came with it on Adoons's wound, bandaged it, and gave him one of the painkiller pills we were issued with.

"I would be a good shepherd for you. It is easy to work well for a kind master. Anyone can see baas will give good food, and a hut with a proper roof, and no sjambok whippings. Except for checky young men who have been to school."

"Come on, we must find a shelter for the night,"

I said. I didn't like the thought of the hyenas he had talked about.

"These pills are good. The pain is quiet. Baas is like a doctor, eh? A sheep farmer has to be a doctor. I am very good with karakul ewes at lambing time. Baas knows, for the best fur you must kill the lambs as soon as they are born. Stillborn lambs are better. Their skins shine like black nylon with water spilled on it. It's messy, clubbing and skinning the little things without damaging the pelts. It's sad to hear all those ewes baaing. The meat is only fit for crows and vultures. But the rich ladies want the pelts before they get woolly."

He pointed out an overhanging rock twenty yards away. "Shall we spend the night there? Out of the dew, and it's open only on one side."

As we moved, I picked up dry sticks for kindling, but he put his hand on my arm. "If the soldiers see me in the firelight, or my people see baas, they will shoot."

I felt foolish and amateur.

"The dead men have clothes. Shall I fetch some?"

"We'll go together," I said. I wasn't going to get myself ambushed.

We went round the rock to the little cliff where the bodies lay. He whistled in admiration. "Baas shoots like a machine. These dead Ovambos look as if they've been arranged with a forklift truck." He added proudly, "I can drive a forklift. I learned on the sheep ranch."

We collected a couple of goatskins, a bush shirt with only a small blood patch, a water bottle, and a haversack of boiled ears of corn. There were three rifles. I grabbed two and took the bolts out of them. Adoons had already taken possession of the third. He grinned mischievously as he worked the bolt and demonstrated how he could use the rifle by tucking its butt under his sound arm.

"Now we can help each other, eh, baas. Like that bird that sits in a crocodile's mouth and cleans bits of meat out from between the crocodile's teeth. The crocodile does not eat him."

We settled down close together under the over-hand and had an ear of corn each, and a pull from my hip flask. My dear old ma gave it to me when I was leaving for the border. "When you put it to your lips, it is your old momma kissing you," she said. I wondered what she would say if she knew she was kissing a Swapie Hottentot, too.

"Angora goats pay better than karakul sheep in the Dry Veld," Adoons said. "When I am the head shepherd, baas will give me a few sheep of my own. I will have a woman with buttocks that stick out so much you can use them for a stepladder. Ai! What fat yellow legs that woman has!" He sucked his breath in lasciviously. "Baas will have white girls in town but on the farm now and then a bushman girl. Ai, what a surprise he gets when he finds that the girl has an apron!" He described in detail the strip of skin some bushman women have hanging down from their gashes, and how some bushmen have an erection all the time, just like in the rock paintings.

I got sleepy and he shook me. "No sleep tonight," he said. "Listen." There were sounds of animals round the bodies. "Better we talk. Also it is good for a man and his mate to chat, isn't it?"

"I thought you fellows didn't want white men to have farms," I said. "You want all the land for yourselves."

"Oh, yes. Yes, that's right. General Kareo says I will have a farm of my own. And a hundred sheep."

"Why stop at a hundred? Why not a thousand? Be a big boss. Make people call you 'Mr. Adoons.' "

"How will I look after a thousand animals? I

can't even count past twenty sheep without taking stones out of one pocket and putting them in the other. No, not a thousand. Unless—unless baas was my foreman." He laughed like a drunkard. "If my people win the war, will baas be my foreman? Please. Baas could have the big farmhouse and a motorcar. Baas need not call me 'baas,' just 'Mr. Adoons.' Everything my foreman wants to do, he can do. Will my foreman be angry if some of the shepherds hide away when the police visit?"

"If your lot were the government, they would be your policemen."

"Policemen are policemen. Dogs' turds. Always after passes."

"Your lot say there won't be passes anymore."

"No passes! If people don't have passes, how can you trace a stock thief? What will we do if bad Ovambo kaffirs steal my karakuls?"

"That's your problem. Perhaps you'll have to get fierce German guard dogs."

"Oh, yes. That's a clever idea. My foreman will always find a way. Now, let's talk of nice things, not problems. What is baas's name?"

"Martinus."

"That is a friendly name for a foreman. In the evenings, after the shepherds have done their work and the sheep and goats are in their thorn kraals, Mr. Adoons and Foreman Martinus will sit together and talk and look at the veld. Ai, it's pretty country, between Platberg and the Boa River. Short sweet grass and big flat-crown thorn trees for shade. Animals eat the pods in the winter. There are eland and koodoo and impala and bushpigs, but enough grass for karakul sheep too."

"Sounds all right," I said.

"In the kloof there are wild bees and baboons. Ai, those baboons! When a baboon finds a marula tree where the plums have fermented, he gets as drunk as a man. Ai, those drunk baboons! The leopards eat only baboons, never sheep."

"Any water?"

"Water! There is the Boa River and big freshwater pans full of barbel and eels and ducks, and widow birds with long black tails like church deacons, and spur-wing geese on the mud flats. The place is called Raraba. We shall sit and drink buchu brandy and talk. Or just sit silent, like old friends do."

"What the hell would you and I find to talk about?"

"Ai, pals' talk. About the grazing and the government and women and hunting and what happens after you die. I suppose baas knows lots of Jesus stories."

"I don't like buchu," I said.

"Do you like the kind of brandy called Commando? They say it is good."

"Klipdrif is the best kind."

"Then we will have Klipdrif, Martinus."

"If it's hot and dry, one could irrigate a few acres for a vineyard," I said.

"Does Martinus know about wine?"

"My grandfather used to make wine with grapes from his backyard."

"Ai, but this is lucky! So Foreman Martinus would grow grapes and make sweet wine. They say if you give a girl a bottle of that red Cape wine, her legs open before the bottle is finished. But I like brandy better."

"Me too," I said.

"Sometimes we will give a bottle of wine to the old people, too. On Mr. Adoons's farm the labourers can stay even when they are too old to work. And when the rations are given out, the old people get meat and mealie meal, too, just like the others. Is that right, Martinus?"

"If the baas says so," I said.

At first light we stretched and scouted. There was no activity. Adoons tore a sleeve out of a dead guerrilla's shirt; I made a sling and tied his wounded arm against his chest. He kept a grip on the rifle all the time.

I offered him my flask, and we each took a swallow. He handed me one of the two ears of corn left in the haversack, and pointed south. "Foreman Martinus must walk that way. I will go north."

"Good luck, Mr. Adoons. I'll come and visit you at your farm at Raraba after the war, and see if you still need a foreman."

"Ai, Martinus," he said, "we will drink and talk, eh. Ai, how we will talk!" He knocked his rifle barrel against mine, like clinking a glass, and set off.

I slid behind the rock where I could watch him without exposing myself. Late Dad used to say if you trust a Hottentot you might as well wear a cobra for a necklace; so I kept my crossed hairs on him, expecting him to whirl round any moment and loose off, or to disappear behind a boulder or thick shrub and perhaps circle round to take me in the rear. However, he walked very deliberately up the hill, and did not dodge behind trees or rocks like an experienced veld man would, nor did he look back to see what I was doing.

When he reached the top of the kopje he stood for some moments silhouetted against the sky and waved his gun. Challenging me to shoot? When he disappeared over the top, I quickly shifted to another position a couple of hundred yards away so that if he crawled round to the side of the kopje I would be ready for him. By sunup nothing had happened, so I decided he was on his way to find his band. He would probably keep the field dressing I put on his arm and pretend that he had shot a South African soldier.

I found my chaps easily enough—I told them I could have shot three or four of them if I had been a guerrilla—and sent them to see what they could find on the Swapies I had shot; even those fellows sometimes have letters or helpful papers.

You would think a man's second-in-command would want to say a warm word about the marksmanship. The blackies were impressed, but Johan said, "You shouldn't have shot to kill, Sarge. We're not in the humane hunting business, you know. A dead Swapie is nafi, isn't he?" He liked showing off his intelligence jargon, like using "nafi" to mean "not available for interrogation."

I shut up about Adoons. My blackies might have been able to pick up his trail and perhaps find him before he rejoined his lot, especially if his wound started bleeding again. Then, if they roughed him up a bit, he could hardly avoid giving the whole story away, and that would mean a court-martial for me, wouldn't it?

We eventually caught a few Swapies. I did not like Johan's attitude, but he was right—a dead prisoner is nafi—so I shot for the leg and told the men to do the same. I stood by with a submachine gun at the ready during the interrogations in case any of the prisoners knew about me and Adoons. Fortunately, none did.

When I finished my army I took my discharge there in South-West and went to have a look at the Platberg area and especially Raraba.

It is nice country, if you like desert, and a man could pick up a thousand hectares cheap from fellows who are getting cold feet about the UN. Also the market for Persian lamb—that's kara-kul—is looking up again, now that Greenpeace has stopped women from buying baby seal. Some sheep ranchers say they would send Greenpeace a donation if it wasn't for the currency restrictions.

I followed the Boa River up to Platberg. The river runs against the mountain cliffs, so there is no space in between for a farm. I thought I must have misunderstood Adoons.

That evening there was a drunk lying asleep in the gutter outside the hotel. The doorman laughed when I bent down to shake the man.

"Leave him, mister," he said. "He's happier in Raraba."

It turns out that is what the Hottentots around there call a lullaby, a dreamland that is too nice to be real. At first I was disappointed. Then I thought, Just as well. Suppose a man had a nice sheep ranch, and then one day a bloody old yellow Hottentot pitched up and said, "Martinus, old friend, do you remember your baas, Mr. Adoons? I've brought a bottle of Klipdrif brandy. That's the kind you like, isn't it? Let us sit and drink and talk pals' talk."

It would be embarrassing, eh.

It's Quiet Now

Gcina Mhlope

Everyone seems to be going to bed now. The rain is coming down in a steady downpour, and I don't think it's going to stop for a long time. Normally I would be joining the others, going to bed while it's still raining so that I can enjoy the sound of it while I wait for sleep to come and take me. I don't want to play any soft music either. I just want to stand here at the window and watch what can be seen of the rain coming down in the dark.

The news in the papers is always the same— some people's house petrol-bombed, youths and activists arrested, suspected informer necklaced, police shootings—it only varies from place to place. It's been like this for . . . I don't know how long. It's really depressing. Today I did not even have to buy a paper, things just kept happening since late this morning.

The PUTCO buses have not been going into the townships. Last week they started coming into our township again. The newspapers said that the local Residents' Association had gone to ask the authorities to bring back the buses, but members of the Association know nothing about it. Most old people seemed quite relieved that the buses were back, but they knew it wouldn't last. Company delivery vans have not been coming in either; the students have burnt so many of them in the past few months.

The house of the local "Mayor" was also burnt down. It was at one o'clock after midnight when we were woken up by two loud explosions one after the other, and soon the house was eaten up by hungry flames. The "Mayor" and his family just made it out of the house, running for their lives. Everything was burnt to ashes by the time the police and fire engines arrived. When I saw his house like that, I remembered what he had said a few weeks back in a Residents' meeting.

"You seem to forget that I am as black as you are, and I suffer just like you do under the apartheid laws of this country." The grumbling from the audience showed that nobody believed him.

A lot of things have been happening here; I just can't keep track. Young children who hardly understand what is really going on are also shouting the slogan "Siyayinyova," which simply means "We will destroy or disrupt."

Nobody was expecting anything today, even though there were more policemen than usual—there have been police driving up and down our streets for quite a while now. We carry on with our work and sort of pretend they are not there.

I was carrying on with my work as well, when I suddenly heard singing. I ran to the window and there, at a school in Eighth Avenue, these children—you know I can still see them as if there's a photograph in my mind. . . . They poured out of their classes into the streets, where the police were. They were shouting "Siyayinyova!" at the tops of their little voices. They picked up rocks and bricks and started attacking buses, company delivery vans and police cars. When the police started chasing them, they ran through double-ups (small paths cutting through people's houses). I stood transfixed at the window. There was running everywhere, just school uniforms all over the township, and shouting and chanting and screaming and burning of policemen's and councillors' houses.

Two company vans were burnt in front of the house right opposite us. The fire jumped and caught on to the house as well, and then there was black smoke from the house and the cars and the cars in the next street and the next. . . . Soon the streets were lost in the dust and smoke.

Clouds from earth began to meet clouds from the sky. We suddenly heard—*ghwara! ghwara!* Lightning and thunder! Louder than any bomb or gun. Poor soldiers, their guns came down as the rain began to fall—*whhhaaaaa.* . . . Maybe it came to clean up the mess.

People started coming back from work. It kept on raining and no one even ran. They walked in the rain as if everything was as they had left it. Some had heard the news from work, and others could see that a lot had happened. But they walked home as usual and got on with their suppers. I didn't have an appetite at supper. I wonder if I should go to sleep now. There is only a light drizzle coming down and all seems quiet in the night.

Glossary

assegai—spear

baas—master (basie, baasie, little master)

bail—tool

biltong—dried meat

bivvie—bivouac; camp

Boer—farmer; used by blacks as a derogatory term for "Afrikaner," though Afrikaners use it with pride

Boeremusiek—Afrikaans folk music

bonnet—hood

boot—trunk

bundu—wilderness, equivalent of "the boondocks"

Bushman—derogatory term for the San Cape aboriginals

catapult—slingshot

Coloured—official term for person of mixed race; many now reject the term, choosing to be called "black"

doek, doekie—headscarf

donga—gully

endorsed out—deported to tribal reserve

Group Areas—the Group Areas Act enforces racial segregation of neighborhoods and has led to massive enforced removals of blacks.

Hottentot—derogatory name for the Khoi-Khoi Cape aboriginals; sometimes a derogatory term for people of mixed race

kaffir—highly insulting, equivalent of "nigger"

klipkop—blockhead, used for blacks

kloof—ravine

koppie, kopje—hill

kraal—African village; farm laborers' compound; animal pen

location—ghetto

mealie—corn

moeroga—wild spinach

munt—derogatory term for black

napkins—diapers

native—derogatory term for black

nkosi—lord (nkosikaas: mistress, chieftainess)

Ovambo—a Namibian national group

palaver—originally a parley between white colonials and African representatives

pap—porridge

piccanin—derogatory term for black child

platteland—rural areas

rand—local currency

shebeen—unlicensed drinking place

sjambok—animal hide whip

stoep—front verandah

Swapie—member of SWAPO (the South West African People's Organization), the Namibia independence movement

veld—open grassland

vetkoek—flat bread fried in oil

vlei—marshy land

Notes on Contributors

Dennis Brutus was born in Southern Rhodesia (now Zimbabwe). He grew up in Port Elizabeth, South Africa, and attended the segregated Fort Hare University College. After serving time for political activities in the Robben Island prison, he went into exile and has been active in the international anti-apartheid movement. His poetry collections include *Sirens, Knuckles and Boots* and *A Simple Lust*. Since 1971 he has lived and taught in the U.S.

Peter Abrahams' "Crackling Day" is from his autobiography, *Tell Freedom*, which ends with his leaving South Africa at the age of 20. His novel *Mine Boy* is about a young man, Xuma, who comes from the country to the slums of Johannesburg, where he finds work in the gold mines and manhood in resistance, and where the girl he loves is destroyed by self-hatred. Abrahams lives in Jamaica.

Doris Lessing was born of British parents in Persia, and grew up from the age of five in Southern Rhodesia (now Zimbabwe). Her books about southern Africa include *The Grass Is Singing*, the first novels in her *Children of Violence* series and *African Stories*, from which this story is taken. She is also the author of *The Golden Notebook* and many other novels and short stories. She lives in London.

Dan Jacobson was born in Johannesburg and grew up in Kimberley in the Cape Province. The author of numerous novels, short stories and essays, he has won several literary awards. His short stories have appeared in *The New Yorker*, *Encounter*, and many other magazines, and have been collected in *A Long Way from London*, from which this story is taken, and *Beggar My Neighbor*. He lives in London.

Nadine Gordimer was born and raised in South Africa and lives in Johannesburg. The winner of numerous international prizes for her novels and short story collections, she lectures frequently in the U.S., Europe and Africa on South African literature and politics. Both stories in this anthology have been dramatized in excellent hour-long films, with screenplays by Gordimer and South African casts and settings.

Zoë Wicomb's story is from *You Can't Get Lost in Cape Town*, a collection of loosely connected, short stories about growing up poor in a township near Cape Town, leaving for England and returning educated and a stranger.

Gcina Mhlope was born in Hammarsdale, near Durban. She is an actress at the Market Theatre, Johannesburg, and has toured Britain, Europe, and the U.S. She won an Obie award for her work in *Born in the RSA* at New York City's Lincoln Center, and in 1988 she staged the American premiere of her play *Have You Seen Zandile?* in Chicago. "I grew up very attached to books as friends," she says. "I was at high school in the Transkei when I started writing poems and stories in Xhosa. I started writing in English much later, when I was already in Johannesburg, using a public toilet as my study room."

Mark Mathabane's story is from *Kaffir Boy: The True Story of a Black Youth's Coming of Age in Apartheid South Africa*. A bestseller in the U.S., the autobiography describes his struggle for survival under conditions of overwhelming brutality and deprivation. In 1979 at the age of eighteen he came to the U.S. on a tennis scholarship.

Ernst Havemann was born in Zululand (now part of Natal), South Africa. He grew up on a South African farm and worked as a mining engineer before becoming a writer. "A Farm at Raraba" first appeared in *The Atlantic* and is one of the stories in his collection *Bloodsong and Other Stories of South Africa.* He lives in Canada.

Acknowledgments

Every effort has been made to trace the ownership of all copyrighted material and to secure the necessary permissions to reprint these selections. In the event of any question arising as to the use of any material, the editor and publisher, while expressing regret for any inadvertent error, will be happy to make the necessary correction in future printings. Thanks are due to the following for permission to reprint the materials listed:

Dennis Brutus for his poem "Somehow We Survive" from *A Simple Lust*. Reprinted by his permission.

Jonathan Clowes Ltd. for "The Old Chief Mshlanga" from *This Was the Old Chief's Country* by Doris Lessing,

Copyright 1951 by Doris Lessing. Reprinted by permission of Jonathan Clowes Ltd., on behalf of Doris Lessing.

Faber & Faber Ltd. for "Crackling Day" by Peter Abrahams. Reprinted by permission of Faber & Faber Ltd. from *Tell Freedom* by Peter Abrahams.

Houghton Mifflin Company for "A Farm at Raraba" by Ernst Havemann, from *Bloodsong and Other Stories of South Africa* by Ernst Havemann. Copyright © 1987 by Ernst Havemann. Reprinted by permission of Houghton Mifflin Company.

Dan Jacobson for his story "A Day in the Country." Reprinted by permission of the author.

Macmillan Publishing Company for "The Road to Alexandra" by Mark Mathabane. Reprinted with permission of Macmillan Publishing Company from *Kaffir Boy* by Mark Mathabane. Copyright © 1986 by Mark Mathabane.

Peake Associates for "The Toilet" and "It's Quiet Now" by Gcina Mhlope. Reprinted with permission of Peake Associates. These stories were originally published in *Sometimes When It Rains: Writings by South African Women*, edited by Ann Oosthuizen, Pandora Press.

Random House, Inc., for "When the Train Comes" from *You Can't Get Lost in Cape Town* by Zoë Wicomb. Copyright © 1987 by Zoë Wicomb. Reprinted by permission of Pantheon Books, a division of Random House, Inc.

Simon & Schuster, Inc., for "The Old Chief Mshlanga" by Doris Lessing. Reprinted from *African Stories* by Doris Lessing. Copyright © 1951, 1953, 1954, 1957, 1958, 1962, 1963, 1964, 1965 by Doris Lessing. Reprinted by permission of Simon & Schuster, Inc.

Viking Penguin Inc. for "A Chip of Glass Ruby" from *Selected Stories* by Nadine Gordimer. Copyright © 1961 by Nadine Gordimer; "Country Lovers" ("Town and Country Lovers: Two") from *A Soldier's Embrace* by Nadine Gordimer. Copyright © 1975 by Nadine Gordimer; the quotation beginning "It's about suffering . . ." from *Burgher's Daughter* by Nadine Gordimer. Copyright © 1979 by Nadine Gordimer. All rights reserved. All selections reprinted by permission of Viking Penguin, a division of Penguin Books USA, Inc.

HAZEL ROCHMAN was born and raised in South Africa, where she worked as a journalist. She left Johannesburg for England in 1963, and the following year, the South African authorities withdrew the passports of her husband and herself. She taught high school in London, and in 1972 she and her husband moved to Chicago, where they live with their two sons. A graduate of the University of Chicago, she worked for eight years as a junior high school librarian and high school librarian at the University of Chicago Laboratory Schools.

Ms. Rochman is now an assistant editor at ALA *Booklist*, where she reviews books for young adults (and nearly everything on South Africa). She is the author of TALES OF LOVE AND TERROR: *Booktalking the Classics, Old and New*, and has had reviews and articles published in many national journals, including *The New York Times Book Review*, *School Library Journal*, and *The Horn Book*. She has appeared as a frequent guest on Chicago public radio, discussing books for young adults.